NoLab

NoLab

a novel

Richard Roth

Owl Canyon Press

First Edition, 2019
All Rights Reserved
Library of Congress Cataloging-in-Publication Data

Roth, Richard.
NoLab —1st ed.
p. cm.
ISBN: 978-0-9985073-8-5
2019946083

Owl Canyon Press
Boulder, Colorado

This is a work of fiction. Names, characters, businesses,
places, events, locales, and incidents are either the products
of the author's imagination or used in a fictitious manner.
Any resemblance to actual persons, living or dead, or actual
events is purely coincidental.

"I'd swap my horse and dog for you" is a lyric from the
song, "Sioux City Sue," written by Ray Freedman and Dick
Thomas in 1945.

For Susan

"I'd swap my horse and dog for you."

1

You may have heard of me, Ray Lawson. I'm the artist who got arrested eighteen years ago for practicing medicine without a license. I was led away in handcuffs, spent the night in jail, and was subjected to a humiliating court case. The charges never stuck, but my associate, Dr. Albert Moore, did suffer serious consequences. The media were relentless, over the top, and deliberately misleading. I became a bit player in someone else's movie.

What I actually did was quite simple—I created drugs that elicited specific user experiences. Each pill was a miniature work of art designed to alter perception.

The art objects we so carefully construct are created to provide viewers with experiences. The nature and quality of the experience may be endlessly debated, but it is ultimately the experience that counts. In any case, I simply eliminated the middleman. Why do we need those cumbersome chunks of stone or paint-encrusted canvases if we can get right to the experience without all the effort?

Being a product of the 60s, I imagine, had a lot to do with the mindset that led me to create drugs that would activate specific neurological receptors. No massive welded steel structure required, no multimillion dollar film production, just one little pill, in your bloodstream and inside your head. So neat, so minimal, so efficient.

I include here Gene Fleming's *Times* review of *Nitro*, my first exhibition of pharmaceuticals.

Raymond Lawson's work is a frontal assault on art as we know it. What is one to make of this spare exhibition? Just eight vitrines, each housing a minuscule geometric form, like a jewel or some rare particle from deep space—a cylinder, one-quarter inch in diameter, yellow-green with an exquisite dry matte surface in one—a half-inch red and white capsule in another. Each work, pill actually, takes its title from the name of a roller coaster: Viper, Corkscrew, Vortex, Tidal Wave, Cyclone, Predator, Mean Streak, *and* Nitro. *At first glance, they are simply minimal artworks in miniature, but Lawson is up to more mischief than that. These little forms are not as harmless as they appear. They are psychopharmaceuticals, made to be ingested, and designed to create unique experiences in the user. Each piece is available as an edition of two, and the buyer must obtain a prescription from the neurologist who collaborated with Lawson on this project. Presumably, the collector who purchases an edition ingests one pill and can exhibit the other or hold it as an investment. Lawson's pill-works are said to utilize stimulants, psychedelics, tranquilizers, and empathogens. The various experiences include euphoria, hallucinations, an altered sense of time, and a momentary lapse of memory that according to the catalog copy induces "a state of mind-boggling nowness." I know not whether the claims made for this work are true, and the beauty is, it doesn't matter.* Nitro *would make Duchamp smile. Ray Lawson has stirred up a whole mess of conundrums and, with great wit and style, comments wickedly on the true religion of our time—pharmaceuticals. This viewer is hooked and I haven't truly experienced the work. I remain drug-free. Pity, no samples for critics.*

Gene Fleming, *The Times*, March 22, 1998

***

August 2016

During my gradual departure from the fray—the personalities and the politics of the art world—I gave up on the pharmaceutical pieces and other conceptual projects and returned to painting. You know the old joke, "Why did the conceptual artist decide to make a painting? Because it was a good idea." The new work is abstract. Severely minimal. As the world looks uglier, I have turned inward. The paintings are more about how my brain works than anything out there in the world. Not unlike my pill pieces, if you think about it. Hey, there's a big uncharted world inside your head, deeper, richer, more resistant to navigation than the Mariana Trench.

I am happy to report that my life is pretty normal now, relatively speaking. I teach a few days a week at Columbia and spend the rest of my time in the studio. It's a sublimely introspective and productive moment, free of the strident, emotional, rough and tumble ideological conflicts of my past.

NoLab

With two longtime friends, fellow misfits in academia—Nina Spalding and Victor Florian—an ill-mannered confederacy was established. Nina is smart and attractive. One of the rare academic women who wears makeup, dresses in clothing too tight, and curses with enviable fluidity. Her students love her. On a particularly glorious Friday, the three of us made our way to the wilds of New Jersey for our annual anthropological lunch expedition. I felt myself relaxing into a welcomed lighthearted conviviality.

"Packaging is everything!" Victor announced over gyros at the Parthenon, a grand and classic Jersey diner. "Take a naked woman. Pretty nice, yes? But really, when you come right down to it, you know, a naked woman is not all that great." Nina and I paused, mouths agape, as we waited for the bomb to drop. You could always depend on Victor to say the most outrageous, culturally insensitive, but ultimately insightful things. He was a wild man from the last generation of artists who lived real lives and then fell into art. Dogmatic, passionate, MFA-less, he was completely refreshing. After many years teaching sculpture, he was soon to retire.

Victor continued, "Have her put on some frilly little underthings, some panties, and a little lace bra and then you have something! Yes! Something very complex, no? Something intoxicating. Packaging is everything!"

Nina winced and said, "Well…yes, packaging is damned important. I remember when I was a student, there was a life drawing class…we were encouraged to ask the model to take specific poses. One day, just as the class was beginning and before the model changed out of her street-clothes, one student asked the model to leave her panties on for the day's pose. This little stretch of black nylon caused quite a fuss. The model, a woman in her thirties, hesitated but finally agreed. A few students objected on the grounds that it was exploitative and kinky. But the student who made the request argued that it couldn't be kinky as the model was less naked."

"It's odd, but it seems more wholesome, clinical even, to draw a completely naked person in that context," I suggested. "The studio model is a body with sexual characteristics but without sexuality, and without a personality. Introduce a small article of clothing that increases the model's physical privacy, and you end up exposing her. You change her from a *body in art school* to a *woman*—and that can turn a life drawing class upside-down."

"Panties problematize perception. Therefore panties are art," Victor proclaimed. "They increase the amount of pleasure and wonderment in the world."

"Victor, you *are* a genius—*packaging is everything*," Nina exclaimed. "Hey, but seriously, the real perversity is that we're still using nude models to teach art. Hello? What century is this?"

"Amen! And please pass the fucking ketchup," said Victor.

"You know Maurice is in the hospital," I said.

"Yeah I heard. Is it bad?" asked Nina.

"They don't know. Still doing tests, some kind of

blockage…"

"Christ! Let's not go there. I'm eating."

"Remember the faculty meeting when Fiddich headed to the blackboard to lay out one of his typical, long-winded, mind-numbing grievances. You know, with lists and diagrams…" said Nina.

"Yeah, yeah, Maurice jumped over a desk and beat Fiddich to the blackboard, and actually ate the frigging chalk," I said.

"And everyone started whooping and applauding," said Nina.

"Good fucking days," said Victor.

"I think Maurice is a lot smarter than we ever acknowledged," I said. "He used to tell his students this ridiculously simplistic little folk tale that I kind of just ignored. Now I've come to see it as searingly insightful."

"Better than the number one most important design principle of all time?" said Nina.

"What the hell can that be?" said Victor.

Nina said, "Victor, you are so…so…"

"Ignorant," I said.

"Well if you're so smart, what is this exalted design principle?" said Victor, looking at me.

"Simple, it's unity and variety," I said. "Everyone knows that."

"Yeah, the work needs to be a unified whole, you know—a gestalt, but without variety it's dead."

"Sounds like a cheap trick to me. I don't follow recipes," said Victor.

"Well, Maurice's dictum isn't a recipe or a design principle, it's more philosophical than that."

"We can't stand the suspense," said Nina.

"Okay, Maurice's little allegory went something like this: The world is like an apple. Everyone living on the apple wants to get to the core. They argue about where to dig—the best place to dig to get to the core. Some say it's here, others disagree—insist it's over there. The debate never ends. They don't understand the simple truth—every place is the best. You can get to the core from any starting point. All you have to do is dig deep enough."

"Hmm, not bad, not bad at all. Very Zen, very mythological," said Victor.

"I dig it too. Forgive the pun," said Nina.

"Coffee anyone?" the waitress asked.

"No thanks," said Nina.

"I'll take one," said Victor, "and how about a baklava."

"You got it, hun."

"Is there a federal law requiring Greek diners to display clashing Formica patterns?" asked Victor, looking about. "Let's see… faux wood-grain, a granite pattern. One, two different faux marble patterns. Blue and white walls with specks of gold, and a boomerang pattern on the counter. Ouch!"

"And don't forget the smoky veined mirrors and fluted fiberglass columns," I said.

Victor finished his coffee and, though he didn't offer, Nina and I ate most of his baklava. "Order your own next time. You two are so fucking rude."

Victor's phone rang. It was his son, Corey. Nina yelled, "Hi Cor." While Victor spoke, Nina went outside for a cigarette. I dealt with the check and visited the restroom. By the time I exited the Parthenon, Nina and Victor were arm wrestling on a workbench behind the restaurant. Nina's lit cigarette rested on the edge of a fifty-five gallon drum. No one could beat Victor in arm wrestling, but that didn't stop Nina from going all out. Her face was red and the veins of her neck were bulging. Standing behind Nina, I grabbed her hand with both of mine and pushed down against Victor's superior force. With my full weight in play, Nina and I slowly downed the old man. Nina hooted and gave me a high five. I said, "Okay, children, let's go back to the real world."

2

After teaching my Tuesday grad class, I headed to my loft in the East Village, a large but rundown space where I've lived and worked for the past eleven years. As usual, I took the subway downtown to Astor Place. Exiting with the crowd, I pushed against a stubborn turnstile till it burped me out on the other side. I ran up the stairs through a pungent fog of urine. Headed east. At the cube across from Cooper Union, a heavily tattooed man with a live boa constrictor was offering a small crowd the opportunity to pose for pictures with the snake. "For a mere ten dollars, my friends." It was a truly magnificent creature, with a pattern of brown ovals and extraordinary shapes between—a survivalist's lesson in figure/ground relationships. The snake had to be at least eight feet long. The exotic alien appeared regally calm as it was placed on the shoulders of a plump woman wearing a zebra patterned dress.

I never tired of what I witnessed on those streets. Lower Manhattan was my Yosemite, my Galapagos, my Sahara. My La Scala, my Prado, my Bodleian. Every day was a revelation.

I stopped to pick up dinner at one of the few remaining Ukrainian butcher shops in the East Village. Walked by rows of old tenements—each one emitting a unique aroma. The walk home was a transnational culinary expedition. I entered my building—the lone industrial structure on the block—got the mail and headed upstairs. The light was out in the landing, as usual. Had to use the flashlight on my cell phone to find the lock. As I juggled the phone, the keys, and my bag of kielbasa, I heard something behind me. Breathing? A cough? A grunt? Oh fuck! After all these years, it's finally my time. Time to get shivved. Bludgeoned. Shot. The obituary will read: "Raymond Lawson, artist known for his controversial exhibitions of drugs, found dead in a pool of congealed blood." And for what? For my phone? My credit card? For the few bucks in my pocket? I couldn't summon the courage to turn around. I waited for the blow to my head, the whoosh of the straight razor, the burn of the bullet. But, nothing happened. Maybe I just imagined it all. Then I heard footsteps, no doubt about it. Finally, in the darkness, I turned to face my destiny. A voice said, "Ray—Ray it's me, Pinky."

"Pinky!——Jesus Christ! You scared the hell out of me! What the hell?"

"Need to talk."

"Jesus!"

"Calm down, Ray."

"Need to talk…uh…okay. Jesus! Come in. Come in."

Stuart "Pinky" Goldstone was the father of an ex-grad student, Jeffrey Goldstone. I was Jeff's advisor in 2001. That's when Jeff started hanging out with two other precocious grads—Kaylee Boone and Dave Collins—all highly adept at testing limits. They formed a collaborative group and christened it NoLab. Because of my early psychopharmaceutical pieces and the highly publicized court case that followed, and because I taught all the oddball courses—like *Bumu Culture*, a graduate studio class in which the students worked to create fads, booms, and other short-lived popular phenomena—the three gravitated to me.

During that time I was especially close to my MFA student advisees. They fed me with their crazy energy and their optimism. I got to know Pinky when Jeff and his cohorts got into serious trouble with the university and I was summoned to speak on their behalf. Not easy, explaining conceptual art to the president, provost, and head of university security, not easy, especially because NoLab's little art project bordered on mail fraud. They created a pseudo-religion and called it the Church of the Holy Spiral.

According to Church doctrine, God left his fingerprint on the head of every newborn human. The resulting impression is the hair whorl and God's fingerprint is a spiral. Proof that God has touched each and every one of us. The Church advertised an offer inviting adherents (all people were automatically members of the Church) to send in photographs of their whorls plus one hundred dollars. Each responder, in return, would receive a certificate of Divine Birth from the Archpriest of the Holy Spiral and a prophecy. Double whorls were good—touched twice by the Creator; counterclockwise whorls signified interference by Dark Forces, and of course required an additional monetary contribution. Along with contributions, responders often attached heartbreaking stories about drug use, lost opportunities, and runaway children. NoLab received tens of thousands of dollars in the mail. It all went straight to their pockets. Jeff referred to the contributors as "pathetic imbeciles, born to be duped." After a number of complaints, the U.S. Postal Service investigated NoLab, and the University was notified. The Postal Service ordered NoLab to cease and desist. Then the University held a disciplinary hearing. The NoLab members weren't expelled. Due more to the fact that Pinky was a big donor to the university than to my help with their defense, the three got off with a stern warning. Needless to say, Pinky was happy, and Pinky could express happiness in a big way. He's the CEO of Goldstone Technologies Group; his net worth is in the billions.

It looked like Pinky'd been sleeping with his suit on. His comb-over was sticking straight up on the right side. *Jeez. What've we got here?* I wondered.

"How about joining me for a humble dinner, Mr. Goldstone?"

"Sure, Okay, I'll have a bite."

I put the kielbasa in a frying pan. Poured two large vodkas. We toasted, "Cheers!" "Santé!"

"How's Jeff?" I asked.

"That's just it. That's why I'm here. I need your help. Jeff and his NoLab friends have been missing for over two weeks now. Two weeks without a phone call or an email!" Pinky sounded genuinely shaken. "That alone wouldn't be so alarming, but there are…other…contributing factors."

"Is that why you look a mess, hid in the dark hallway and scared the bejeezus out of me? What if I had a gun? I could have killed you." In reality, about all I could have done was whack him with a bag of kielbasa. "What were you thinking? Are you okay? What the hell is going on?"

"Don't worry, I'm okay. Just under a lot of pressure lately. And now with Jeff missing, and my wife badgering me to find him, I'm just overwhelmed. Too complicated to explain. Just a lot going on."

"Well, you look like hell, and right now, to tell you the truth, I'm more worried about you than about Jeff and NoLab."

"Relax, just hear me out, please. You know I lost a lot of friends and colleagues on the top floors of the North Tower. 9/11 was the worst fucking day ever, in New York history, and in my life, and I wasn't even near the World Trade Center that day. I was glad we bombed Iraq. Didn't care if the Iraqis were responsible or not. I think I had a nervous breakdown, but— and this is so weird—Jeff was all fired up. He saw the destruction of the twin towers as some kind of artwork—said it was 'political, cunning, ironic, and'—what else?—yes…'media savvy'. Where did I go wrong with this kid? I mean, I love him, but he's got some really sick ideas. Since 9/11, my relationship with Jeff has never been the same, but at least we've always kept in touch. Now, Jeff's apartment is empty—no Jeff, no communication, no NoLab. I'm terrified they might be planning something crazy. So, I'm here to ask you to help me find my boy."

"You're not worried that he might be in danger?"

"Well, maybe that too."

"I can gather up some names of old classmates, spread the word, whatever." I left the table to get the kielbasa, brought it back on two plates. "Here, it's the best I can do."

"Actually, this looks amazing. I just realized how damned hungry I am."

We sat at the table, a plain, wood door that rested on two sawhorses in the center of my loft. There weren't any rooms or dividing walls, just one large open space with my gear scattered about—cardboard boxes, chairs, and worktables crowded with jars of paint and brushes, everything out in the open, even the bed. The walls were filled with my paintings and paintings in progress—stark and pure, everything I can't achieve in life. These paintings are not the best of me—they're better than me—richer, deeper, smarter than I could ever be. That's the paradox of painting, sweet vulnerable painting. We drank more vodka and ate kielbasa with mustard, nothing on the side, just a forlorn sausage on each plate.

"I know I'm sounding meshuga, but really, I'm fine, *and* I'm not just asking you for some useful information, I'm asking you to find Jeff and NoLab for me. You'll be very well compensated, of course," said Pinky.

"You know, Jeff's not alone in recognizing the strategic brilliance of the 9/11 attack. Remember the German composer Karlheinz Stockhausen's infamous assertion: 9/11 was 'the greatest work of art that is possible in the whole cosmos.' However, acknowledging the sophistication of 9/11 need not negate one's disgust with the monstrosity of the act. I sympathize with your anxiety, but...Pinky, you know very well that I'm just an artist with absolutely no experience in such matters. Why don't you just do the obvious—call the police or hire a private investigator?"

Pinky was very persistent. He said, "You guys were close, and you still have a unique insight into the group's motives. You know their colleagues, their circle of friends. You are the only teacher Jeff ever looked up to. You can find them, I know it."

"I can't do it, Pinky. I wouldn't know where to begin. You can afford the top P.I.s in the world. That's your best bet."

"I would do anything to protect Jeff, anything, but my suspicions have to be completely confidential. Right now I can't trust the private security establishment."

"Yeah, why's that?"

"It's a long story, Ray. Just an inconvenient time for the company to have outsiders poking around. Trust me on this."

"I don't think I'm up to it. It's a big project."

"Just give it a month of your time and let's see how it goes."

"Let me think about it."

"Of course. Sleep on it. Whatever."

"If I take it on I'd require support...an assistant, and...

probably a tech person. I'm sure we'd need to travel..."

"Ray, you can have anything you need."

Pinky thanked me and shook my hand a bit too vigorously. He seemed wobbly so I offered to call him a car.

"No, no, my driver is waiting for me on the corner."

"You have a car here, and you camped out in my dark, stifling hallway! Why didn't you wait in your air-conditioned limo?"

"I wanted to get your attention."

***

The following day, a contract arrived via courier. Pinky made me an offer—one hundred thousand dollars—upfront, no obligation other than a serious effort on my part. In addition, Pinky would cover all expenses, including a fee for a partner. He already had a Lloyd's account established with my name on it. If I took this on I would be entering into something way over my head. Then I thought about my future: aging alone in my decaying loft, and all the diseases that are preparing to afflict me. Yes, all the indignities that await. Senility, Alzheimer's, tumors. Ah yes, the tumors.

Today's cancer patients are advised: *Visualize your immune system attacking your tumor. Imagine white blood cells devouring the alien intruder.* It's supposed to be therapeutic. I guess it's like rooting for the home team. Well, good luck to all so afflicted. I am also into visualization, but definitely not what the doctor ordered. I have *not* been diagnosed with cancer, nonetheless I visualize a tumor growing somewhere deep down in my gut, in my liver, or in my colon perhaps. I imagine it to be the result of some genetic mutation or the consequence of a random calamity or perhaps, plain old environmental assault. In any case, *my* tumor is enjoying its good fortune—it's thriving, doing its thing, pulsating with delight. I see its cells silently multiplying in their dark, damp pocket of flesh, its membranes stretching, clumps breaking off and migrating to new anchorages, the better to generate colonies. *Frenzied entrepreneurs, fat on mitosis, seek market diversity.*

3

If I took on Pinky's project, I would need help. Victor immediately came to mind. Yes, 'packaging is everything' Victor. Victor is smart, not scholarly smart—street smart. He's also fearless. He's a Vietnam vet, half Jewish, half Italian, and was a welder and dock-builder before turning to sculpture. Victor's work evolved into something akin to material science. Though not very successful in crass art world terms, he's the real deal and is increasingly noticed and respected.

Victor's an old lefty, an advocate of workers' rights as well as of the downtrodden everywhere. And, he has an uncanny knack for spotting sexual couplings. Riding together on an elevated train in Brooklyn last year, Victor spied a man and woman screwing in a tenement window, and once, over lunch in Tompkins Square Park on a perfect summer day, he pointed out two ladybugs going at it in the grass. Two ladybugs for Christ's sake! These little orange dots were completely invisible to all. Except to Victor that is. He has the eye. What more could anyone want in an investigative partner?

After reading Pinky's contract three times, I called Victor. He agreed to meet me to discuss the search for NoLab. Decided on

McSorley's—for old time's sake.

Many years ago we drank a lot of ale in McSorley's, its sawdust floor reeking of fermentation. Basically, it's pretty much unchanged today, but it was definitely not a tourist attraction in the 70s. With saltines served in wax paper sleeves straight from the carton, we scarfed down cheddar cheese, raw onions, and hot mustard. McSorley's was *men only* since well before John Sloan painted it in 1912, but in 1970 it was "liberated."

By 5 p.m. we were in McSorley's. I explained the visit from Pinky and his distress concerning Jeff's disappearance. I told Victor about Pinky's disheveled appearance and his odd behavior, his need for confidentiality, his inability to fully explain the reason for his anxiety, and, finally, his substantial monetary offer. Not surprisingly, Victor had many things to say.

"Ray, do you really want to know what I think? This is a hopeless project. I think Pinky is playing you—somehow, someway. Too much money in play. It doesn't smell right. But—I'm an asshole. I volunteered to fight in Nam, another immoral and ill-advised venture with no exit plan. So, what the hell, count me in, but for one month only. Fifty thousand dollars up front plus expenses."

"I hear you *and* I agree that something's a bit shady, but if we play it smart we can get the job done quickly and stash away some cash. And…yes to the 50K."

"Do you know why I'm gonna do this?"

I said, "I think I know. Is it for Corey?"

"Yes, if I didn't have Corey's future to worry about, I

wouldn't go near this job."

"Understood, my friend."

"Why are you doing it?" Victor asked.

"Hmm, not really sure, but…well, to be honest, I guess it's just for the adventure. I like my routine; it's productive, but, you know, *it's a routine*…might be good to escape for a while."

"I think you're lonely."

"Ha!—Maybe."

"So, do you have time for some strategizing and one more round?"

"Sure, one more round."

"Where to begin?" asked Victor.

"I think we have to start by talking to the parents and friends of Kaylee and Dave. Like, did anyone have contact, did anyone file a missing-persons report and, if not, why?"

"That makes sense, but that's exactly what I'm talking about. Why didn't Pinky do this already? Or did he? It's so basic and so easy. Doesn't require hundreds of thousands of dollars."

"Yeah, but 100K to Pinky is what a C-note is to us."

"A C-note?"

"Yes, a C-note."

"What's a C-note?"

"You're kidding right?"

"No."

"You never watched Cagney movies?"

"Yeah, I heard the term. I know it's a big bill, just never knew which one."

"Jeez. It's a hundred dollar bill."

"Yeah, right."

"Anyway, I'm gonna take Pinky at face value: he's worried Jeff is up to something dangerous with NoLab, that's all, and that's fine with me," I said.

"Okay, it's been established, we're doing the search. We can each understand it in our own way, right? Now, let's see…what else do we need to do to get started?"

"You can interrogate Pinky if you like."

"Good idea, but I don't think I want to subject myself to that." Victor paused, then said, "Since you know Kaylee's dad, you should definitely speak to him, what's his name?"

"Niles…Niles Boone," I said. "Well, I haven't been in touch with him forever, but I'll definitely call him. Victor, the only thing resembling a lead that Pinky could provide was NoLab's relationship to what he said was 'some new Midwestern institution.' And, this past year I heard gossip about a new mega -museum somewhere in the hinterlands—of course I didn't pay much attention to it—but, you know, that could be what Pinky was referring to."

"That seems important, but I've no idea how to pursue it," said Victor.

"Let's both work on it. Pinky thinks NoLab's disappearance might have something to do with this phantom organization. It's our only real lead at the moment."

I was startled by a not unpleasant tingling on my upper thigh. It was my phone. Grace Germain, my lawyer, informed me that a collector who'd purchased at least a dozen of my psychopharmaceutical pieces over a decade ago was just now experiencing debilitating symptoms that he contends are the result of ingesting my work. Rashes, blurred vision, memory loss, insomnia, and prolonged crying spells for Christ's sake. Grace said we would easily beat this, as the collector was now seventy-eight and had a history of cocaine use and other unhealthy habits that could explain his alleged ailments. She said it was nothing to worry about—it'll be easy to shake him off. So why was I worried? Because it will cost me time and money, but more importantly, it will be embarrassing. I sure as hell didn't need any more of that kind of attention.

And, I'm still hurting from the harm inflicted on my good friend, Albert Moore, the gentle doctor who wrote prescriptions for all my pill pieces. He was ordered to pay a steep fine by a judge who never heard of irony, and his medical license was suspended for a year. Al never fully recovered from the disgrace.

I mistakenly thought the turmoil surrounding the pill pieces was behind me. Why can't history just stay where it belongs?

***

Back in my loft, I read Pinky's contract one more time, grabbed a pen and signed. I included Victor's participation, and had it couriered back to Goldstone Technologies. Two hours later I got a text message informing me that my new Lloyd's account was credited in full. Victor received a text as well. Pinky thinks we know something critical to the search. Victor and I were ready to do some sleuthing.

***

Fifteen years ago, when NoLab member Dave Collins was a grad student and I was his advisor, I met with him every month or so to discuss his work. On one occasion, there was a young woman in his studio—his girlfriend Kaylee. She was well equipped for art world combat. Multiple piercings dotted the arc of her left ear. A barbed-wire tattoo circled her skinny bicep. She wore ripped jeans and a fuzzy fluorescent-green backpack shaped like a turtle. This bundle of dissonant signs made me smile.

You've got to love art student style. From spiked polychrome hair to elaborately feigned neglect, it's always fun, in your face, and inventive. There are plenty of brilliant, ambitious souls attracted to the arts, and privileged young people who could be anything they want to be. But the aspect of the art world I am most proud to be associated with is its casual acceptance of outcasts and rebels. If you stutter, aren't sure of your gender, are dyslexic, have Asperger syndrome, obsessive-compulsive disorder, A.D.H.D., B.O., or just plain bad attitude, whatever—you're welcome. Everyone's welcome. You can't say that about a lot of disciplines.

As Dave made quick introductions and excused himself to get his work ready for a crit, Kaylee and I made obligatory small talk. I asked her where she was from.

"New York, but now I'm in grad school in Chicago. I'm considering applying here. I *hate* Chicago."

"What kind of work do you do?"

"Conceptual, performance stuff," Kaylee said, then, appearing pleased to think of something else to say, "My father is having a show in Chelsea."

"Really, that's great...what's his name?"

"Oh, you wouldn't know. He's not like famous or anything."

"Come on, try me," I said.

After hesitation and a little more coaxing, Kaylee revealed the name of her artist father. Niles Boone.

"No!"

"Yes," Kaylee said.

"You mean *24-Hour Icons* Niles Boon?"

Kaylee's eyes popped. She must have thought, *how the hell can this guy know about my decidedly obscure artist-father?* I rattled off the names of just about every photo series her father ever made.

When I was a freshman at Cal Arts, Niles Boone was a classmate. After the first year, I transferred to Cooper Union and moved to New York. Niles stayed behind in Valencia. Three years later he showed up to live in New York and we hung out together for a brief period but eventually lost contact.

Niles is a respected conceptual photographer, probably best known for a series of dye transfer prints of items purchased at a 24-hour market. At around 2:00 a.m., he waited near the checkout counter for the most uncanny groupings and then, with the permission of the customer, proceeded to photograph the objects in small groups under a jerry-rigged lighting system on a platform behind the store. The freaky, poetic juxtapositions were awesome. These are the few I still remember (forgive me if my memory is off a bit—but you'll get the idea):

- A box of 100-watt light bulbs, a package of Velveeta slices, and a single coconut.
- An aluminum lawn chair, a quart of 10w30 Penzzoil, a bunch of plantains, a Flintstones watercolor set, and a tube of Preparation H.
- A box of steel wool and a ten-pound bag of ice (my favorite).
- A carton of Camels, frozen corn dogs, a small bottle of Elmer's Glue, and a flea collar.

Kaylee eventually got into our grad program and along with Dave became two-thirds of the infamous NoLab.

***

Adhering to the investigation to-do list Victor and I drew up in McSorley's, I visited Niles to see what he knew about Kaylee's whereabouts. When I called he told me straightaway that he didn't know where she was, but he agreed to meet up. He had a little studio on Twenty-third Street. He welcomed me at the door. His prints were hanging in orderly grids on all the walls. I was surprised to see he was bent over and walked with a cane. We sat down at a large worktable and after catching up on each other's lives, he said, "So you're looking for NoLab."

"That's right. Jeff's dad, Stuart Goldstone, is worried and asked me to help find them. Can you help?"

"Well, Stuart called me a while ago with the same question. I told him just what I'm going to tell you. Kaylee is an independent type. She's thirty-nine years old. She travels a lot and doesn't always tell me where she's going. I really don't worry about her because she's her own person, and besides, we're really not that close. Maybe her mother, my ex, knows something. I have no idea."

"What about Dave's parents? Did you speak to them?"

"I only met his parents once. Don't know if they're still alive. Maybe they're from Canada—I don't remember."

Niles wasn't much help, but I wondered why Pinky didn't tell us he spoke to him?

4

The very first rumor I heard about the Institute was in London late last year at the opening of the "Fundamentalism" exhibition (a big Tate Modern show of ultra-minimal work that included a room dedicated to my early pill pieces). Of course, I didn't know it was called 'the Institute' until later. The rumor had all the earmarks of an urban myth. The Institute sounded threatening, enigmatic, and vaguely mythological. Three months later, back home in New York at a dinner with some painters and dealers, I heard the Institute story again, but this time it was greeted with derision. "It was somewhere in Iowa...or Ohio." "Some billionaire weirdo decided to start his own museum of pop art... or popular culture." "It was going to be the largest museum in the world and—it's in the middle of nowhere."

I called a friend at the Wexner Center. If anyone would know about a new museum in the hinterlands, it would be Felicia. She hadn't heard a peep, though she did mention the Longaberger building in Newark, Ohio that looks exactly like a monumental Longaberger basket—eight-stories tall—Oldenburg on steroids. Many calls later and no leads, I was becoming convinced the Institute was just some internet flotsam. As a last resort, Victor called a friend of a friend in the construction business. "Yeah sure, Carter Wilkinson—the local contractors call him Goldfinger. His Institute is way northwest of Columbus, Ohio." Pay dirt!

***

Carter Wilkinson became our first mission. We flew to Columbus, rented a car and headed north. Exiting I-270 at Hilliard we eventually passed a long progression of strip malls— BP, CVS, Kroger, Jiffy Lube, Wendy's, K Mart, 7-Eleven, Krispy Kreme—then we took a road that sliced through corn and soybean fields.

Victor said, "I love exurbia! Ever notice how the stores get more specialized on these commercial strips as you get farther from the city centers?"

"Not really," I said.

"Well, first you drive by a bunch of auto dealerships in the suburbs, then a store for ATVs and motorcycles, then five miles up the road, into the boonies, you come to a store that only sells batteries—just batteries for Christ's sake. What can possibly come next? You know what—probably a store that just sells battery caps."

"I don't think batteries have caps anymore. They're sealed."

"Well, you get the picture. You know, like you pass a big department store, then a shoe store, then a store that only sells shoelaces, *just* shoelaces, and then you know what comes next?"

"No."

"A store that only sells the little plastic tips on shoelaces. What are they called?"

"Aglets," I said.

"Yeah, yeah, that's it, *just aglets*," said Victor.

Forty-two miles later, driving on progressively narrower roads through a young pine forest, we finally came to a small black and white sign that read simply, "The Institute."

We turned right, between construction barricades, passed perfect cones of sand and gravel, bright green backhoes and chrome yellow Caterpillar bulldozers, down a recently poured ribbon of concrete toward a building still under construction.

We were lucky to have snagged an appointment with Wilkinson. It seems he's a busy man. The guard at the entrance gate greeted us by name and gave us directions. The security was serious and high-tech. Up the winding driveway, the Institute first makes its presence felt as flashes of red between the trees, and then it's on top of you, the most massive box you've ever seen, and it's red, all red, flaming red. It would be easy to imagine cars and construction equipment high off the ground and stuck fast to those red walls. Something as big as the Institute must create its own gravitational pull.

"Fuck me," said Victor.

"'More red is definitely redder than less red.' Barnett Newman would have liked this building."

We parked in the guest zone and walked to the main

entrance. It was a perfect day. The sky was a brilliant blue; three perfectly round clouds floated above the institute like an ellipsis. Passing through the ordinary but oversized industrial door, we were immediately enveloped by a cavernous whiteness.

You might have expected everyone working at the Institute to be in uniform or at least identical coveralls, but no, the stylish woman who greeted us could be a killer Chelsea gallerina.

"Hi, my name is Miyo. Welcome to the Institute. Mr. Wilkinson is expecting you. Please follow me." Her high heels clicked on the concrete floor. She led us on a long walk, past arrays of movable walls, platforms the size of multistory buildings, and massive objects wrapped in plastic. Workers were zipping around on Segways. I couldn't make much sense of what I was seeing. Our guide pointed out one thing on the walk to Wilkinson's office; gesturing toward a rustic wooden shed, she said casually, "the Unabomber shack."

Wilkinson's office is, it seems, a reconstructed Prouvé building. Aluminum, a grid of portholes and those fabulous tapered columns. Inside, all Prouvé furniture. "It's a pleasure and a special thrill to meet you both, two artists I have great respect for. Welcome, welcome! Sit. What can I do for you?" Looking into Victor's eyes, I hoped to receive some signal that would help me decide whether I should disclose our mission right up front or ease into it with small talk, but Victor's face was blanker than a brick. Luckily Wilkinson started talking. "Do you know what I'm up to here?"

"No," I replied, Victor and I shaking our heads from side to side like complete idiots. Miyo offered beverages. We nixed her offer of espresso, accepted mineral water. Wilkinson went on. "You've probably heard rumors—well, we're not going public with anything until everything is more fully resolved. I assume you already discovered that we're flying below the radar. For now, I can say we have a three-part mission. The first and the most conventional activity is collecting and archiving things we consider important from a wide range of culture, but I don't mean art, or at least not art as we presently understand it. In any case, there are more than enough places for art. The archiving and display activities will mostly take place here at the Institute."

"Sounds like you are talking about material culture," said Victor.

"Exactly," said Wilkinson. "We initially intended to exhibit a range of interesting and loaded artifacts: Dr. Kevorkian's euthanasia device, Dolly the cloned sheep—taxidermied, of course, O.J. Simpson's White Bronco, Captain "Sully" Sullenberger's Airbus A320, and the Kaczynski shack, which we already own. Instead, we are now gravitating toward the less *loaded*, the unmarked. Contrary to popular belief, we don't think it's the *great* works of art that shape us. We think it's the daily, ordinary experiences. The vernacular, the quotidian, and the mundane. So, to that end, we've purchased a dozen houses from Levittown and relocated them to the Institute grounds with reconstructed landscaping, sidewalks, driveways, and streets. We are also recreating sets from television game shows and award events. We've already installed *The Wheel of Fortune, The Price is*

Right, Hollywood Squares, and a few amazing sets from Emmy and Grammy award shows. They're pimped-out pinball machines, and no one else is preserving this stuff. They defy design categorization and, of course, they're a modernist's nightmare. I think they predate postmodern architecture, no?"

"It seems like you're collecting from a neglected time period, kind of retro," I said.

"You're right. And that's what we recently decided to depart from. We don't want to go back into the past, now we want to stay in the present and we want to avoid falling into the kitsch trap. As you can see, our program is developing—it's an incredibly exciting process."

A woman entered and Wilkinson stood up immediately. She was extraordinarily striking, pure white hair and blue-green eyes. She wore an elegant gray suit. No jewelry. She said, "I hope I'm not interrupting." Wilkinson said, "No, no, not at all. Ray Lawson, Victor Florian, meet the brains behind this outfit, Ms. Paxinou. She's our Gelson Family Foundation Senior Curator." We nodded hello. "Great to meet you both," she said. "I know your work well. I'm a big fan." She laid a folder down on the table. Wilkinson said to Victor and me, "Please excuse me while I sign a few papers. It'll just take a minute." As he signed, he said, "Oh how I hate to do this." Ms. Paxinou smiled. She picked up the folder and left the room. Wilkinson resumed his explanation of the Institute's mission. "Our second area of interest is probably our most controversial, it's insane actually, but we're completely committed. While we first thought of it as a kind of minor, satellite activity, we are now seeing it as our central focus.

"It's so simple. Artifacts are placed in museums many years after they are made and at great cost because they have become rare, difficult to obtain, and often need restoration that involves extensive research by historians, conservators, and chemists. Consider historical communities like Colonial Williamsburg. Its artifacts are recreated with great difficulty and questionable accuracy. Well, here at the Institute we have decided to jump the gun. We've begun to obtain contemporary institutions we consider to be iconic, and then we simply fix them in time. For example, we just purchased a huge and fairly new Lowes hardware store in Westerville *and* every single thing in it. Every nut, every bolt, every sheet of plywood, twenty-two lawnmower models, and seventy-five chainsaws! All frozen in time circa 2016, and all in context. Nothing has to be replicated. Every inch is authentic."

"I see," said Victor. "You're placing the present in a kind of vacuum till it becomes history."

"Right! Till it becomes the future's history."

"I like that, I like that a lot," I said.

"The third part of our mission is the Foundation. It's also a kind of think tank. It supports the various organizations we're interested in, and it acts in an advisory capacity for the entire institute."

"Does the Foundation support NoLab?" I blurted.

"NoLab," said Wilkinson slowly. "Yes. Yes we have funded

NoLab. Clever devils. The Institute Foundation is presently funding about a dozen small organizations. Why do you ask?"

"We're trying to locate them. They've been missing for weeks."

"That doesn't sound good." Looking toward our greeter, Wilkinson said, "Miyo, please provide Raymond and Victor with a complete copy of our NoLab file."

We chatted on for a while about the Institute and complimented Wilkinson on his ambitious enterprise. It was a serious experiment, one worthy of respect. After all, Victor and I were *all in* on Tibor Kalman's assertion, "Everything is an experiment."

Miyo handed us the NoLab file as we departed.

***

Driving back to Columbus after our visit, Victor and I discussed our meeting with Wilkinson. While I would like nothing more than to impress you with our tough cop-like banter, I must sadly report that Victor and I sounded more like an old married couple gossiping about a dinner party.

Victor read the contents of the file aloud. It contained next to nothing. Just a few pages outlining two innocuously worded grant proposals. "The Information Esthetic" and "Financing the International Art Market." Except for the fact that there *was* a connection between NoLab and the Institute, the file told us zilch.

"After you asked about NoLab, the conversation really dropped off the cliff. He's hiding something. He's a smart one," said Victor. "And Ray, I'm still wondering why Pinky threw that pile of dough at us. It's beyond excessive. There's a lot more going on here than Jeff's alleged disappearance."

"I don't know, Victor, I think we're finally making progress."

"Get real, Lawson. We're inept, even as fake detectives. Pinky knows it and now Wilkinson knows it too. We're being paid to play in some devious game. Something smells."

"Don't be so paranoid. Wilkinson's an interesting guy, and you know, his idea to buy up contemporary iconic institutions and hold them for the future is quite brilliant."

"And audacious," said Victor. "He's like the first fucker who decided to age whiskey. Any normal guy would taste the brew the second week and say, 'Okay, now let's party!' But no, one man thinks the whiskey is getting better every day and decides to wait twelve years to tap the barrel. That man was a crazy, repressed, sick bastard—but also a poet and a genius."

"Freud said civilization was invented by a guy who sublimated his natural urge to urinate on fire, and instead brought the burning embers home for heating and cooking."

"Well, Wilkinson is one sublimated bastard who will die before his collection becomes history," said Victor.

"But really, Victor, why hasn't anyone thought of this before? It makes so much sense."

"Material culture is definitely where it's at," said Victor. "And, Wilkinson may be a deviant, but he *did* hire Ms. Paxinou.

I gotta give him that. Jesus! Never saw anyone move with that kind of grace and elegance. She's definitely an extraterrestrial. Were you as fascinated by her as I was?"

"Fascinated? No, I was completely and hopelessly enchanted. I can't even begin to explain it. How old do you think she is?"

"How old? Does it matter?"

"I'm just curious," I said.

"In her fifties?"

"Well, she *is* beautiful, but it wasn't just that, you know, it was something other than that. She was…"

"On the astral plane," said Victor.

5

Jeff Goldstone was my student fifteen years ago. Since that time, I've followed his career and met up with him at various art events. I remember him as a pretty severe young man, and unpredictable too. One of Jeff's earliest pieces was a very straightforward and seriously well-acted performance of Harold Pinter's *The Homecoming*, straightforward that is with one crazy twist—Jeff added a laugh track appropriated from contemporary TV sitcoms, completely changing the meaning of Pinter's every word. Sitting through Jeff's *Homecoming* was almost unbearable. Its basic structure was that of an assisted readymade. Jeff got quite a bit of attention from this piece and proceeded to use the same device, more or less, on other plays, and later he applied it to some classic films. I always admired the simplicity of it all. It's a device or system that you can apply to anything and everything. Oldenburg—make it larger, Whiteread—cast the negative space, Jeff—add laugh track. The entire universe is just fodder for your generating principal.

Jeff traveled a lot, putting on shows in hip venues till it all got a bit worn. Even the uncanny can become familiar. Between performances, Jeff worked with NoLab. He was the unofficial leader, the radical theorist behind most of NoLab's more questionable activities. Full of himself, super-bright, Jeff always managed to create mayhem.

***

Over ropa vieja, fried plantains, and Modelos in TriBeCa, Victor and I discussed NoLab's disappearance.

As Pinky suggested, the group might be planning a sinister act, an intervention that would make people take notice on a massive scale. NoLab was always complaining about the emptiness of the contemporary art world. *Art today was just expensive home decoration.* Maybe their ideas were immature, but at least they were idealistic. They always said they wanted to do something that *mattered.* They wanted to do more than snag a gallery exhibition—and that *did* deserve support. Yes, there was anger in the group. Deep hostilities sometimes rose to the surface. I *could* imagine a NoLab action that resembled terrorism. So what might such an act be? With Dave and Kaylee's programming expertise it could be a cyber-act. A nasty virus with an ironic twist? Shutting down the internet for a day? Fucking up some military or banking operations? NoLab had the know-how and the hacker connections to do something memorable. And, a cyber-act could be carried out almost anywhere. The Institute could be providing equipment or space.

Victor got a call from his son Corey and took it at the table, motioning to me that it wouldn't be long; I checked my email.

"Hi Corey, how are you? What? Calm down. Just calm down. Hmm, I'll speak to Mr. McCracken tomorrow. I'm sure he's not angry with you. Just relax. I know it wasn't your fault. Where are you now? Good, good, just stay in, watch some TV and get some sleep. I assure you, all will be okay. I love you, Cor. Remember what I told you. Yes, that's right, 'things are never as bad as they seem,' you're the best! I love you. Bye Cor."

Corey has Down syndrome. He's about thirty now, lives in a group home in Queens and has a job doing menial tasks at a supervised facility. He's always calling Victor with job problems, money problems, roommate problems, girl problems. It really breaks my heart. I don't know how Victor can live with this. I think I'd blow my brains out. Corey's mother, Victor's first wife, walked out on both of them a few years after Corey was born, and she never returned.

After the phone conversation, Victor made a note to himself on his cell phone and resumed our discussion right where he left off. The man's a trooper. He asked if some kind of art vandalism was a possibility. No one would be harmed, only pomposity deflated. I didn't think a can of spray paint emptied on a Picasso was NoLab's style. Art vandalism today is nothing but a five-minute sound bite—potatoes too small for NoLab, and pointless as well—better left to the wackos.

At least we succeeded in locating our primary lead—the Institute. Yes, the Institute could be the key. With fading enthusiasm, we decided to hire one of Victor's ex-students, Woody Redman, a bona fide hacker whiz kid, to be on the lookout for online activity that might suggest a NoLab cyber-act. We also decided to pay Woody a visit the following week. He lives on Long Island.

Victor and I were beginning to understand how little we knew about being detectives.

***

Victor never studied art formally. After stints as a welder on bridge jobs and in shipyards, he took on some welding work for a local artist. Eventually he began to make his own sculpture, free-form constructions composed of found steel parts. He loved the lore of the workingman and frequently quoted their folksy braggadocio. "I can weld anything, from a broken heart to the crack in your ass." Bridges, ships, and skyscrapers were Victor's inspiration.

Victor was a fast learner. He read everything, hung out with a group of ambitious young painters, sculptors, and writers, became conversant with Minimalism, Pop, Conceptual Art, and theory. He eventually arrived at a body of work that transcended any ism—it was completely original, really quite brilliant, but was pretty much ignored by an art world that just didn't get it—didn't know how to place it—whatever. None of this phased Victor.

His new work was more akin to material science than to anything you'd think of as sculpture. By pumping air into liquid plastics, he created towering piles of iridescent spheres, like giant clumps of frozen soap bubbles—they were magical. A lot of physics, chemistry, and biology went into these structures. To transform his raw materials, he used chemical infusions, enzyme vats, industrial microwave ovens, heat, and pressure. It hasn't gone unnoticed that this work has a lot in common with molecular gastronomy, but Victor's experiments predated that craze by many years, and Victor did everything on the largest scale possible—these weren't little tabletop pieces, they were room-size. Victor was a kind of mad scientist asking fundamental questions about matter. What would happen if you heated this? Applied pressure to that? Combined these? Nobody in the art world was working this street, and now, in 2016, Victor still stands alone as a manipulator of primary forces. He trusted his generating principles and processes to do all the work, and work they did. Didn't Gaudi say, "Originality is a return to the origin"?

***

I can no longer tolerate art openings and after-parties. Exhibitions look increasingly like the gallery openings depicted in bad Hollywood movies. It's become unbearable, this marketplace of faded signifiers, clichéd representations of transgression and freedom. Nothing's at stake. But who knows, maybe it's just me. I do have a shitty attitude.

I used to participate in all kinds of art events for my career's sake—then for a long blissful time, I just stayed away. However, being the diligent detective, I decided to accept an invitation to an Independent Curators International event to see what I could find out about NoLab's disappearance. I was on a mission! The party was a blue-chip affair in the former Dia space in Chelsea, so definitely worth scoping out, at least I thought so. Victor considered it a waste of time. He went to visit Corey.

Only a pretty good martini and warm reunions with old colleagues could compensate for the inane chitchat with the likes of Grant Slocum, a young dealer who could only be described as deranged. Spotted hyenas have more dignity. He rattled on about the six figures he got for a painting by Mike Ambrose who received his Yale MFA last year. This is the kind of thing that makes the most devoted artists, those passionately in love with art but who feel spiritually homeless in today's art world, simply want to jump ship. Let's be filmmakers, writers, designers. Let's make beer, butcher our own food, repair motorcycles—anything to keep our distance from the Grant Slocums. As Holly Stolz said, "The best artists today are engaged in finding a way *out* of the art world. Escaping—with flair—is the art of our time." Escape artists, I like that! I paint, but am embarrassed to be part of the art world. Eisenhower painted; that's cool, but so did Hitler. Now cats paint, elephants too. Sylvester Stallone and George W. Help!

Finding an excuse to escape Grant Slocum, I headed to the bar for a refill. A prosecco sipping apparition floated by, emerging out of some glorious parallel universe only occasionally visible from our own lackluster one. Ms. Paxinou was more alien and beautiful than I remembered. Her every molecule seemed subtly different than the perfectly delightful molecules of an ordinary beautiful woman.

As a young man in art school, whenever I rode the subway I fell in love with at least three women who just happened to share the car. I don't mean that I was attracted, I mean head over heels in love. A prim young secretary, yellow cashmere sweater, reading a romance novel. A pretty Puerto Rican girl wearing a Catholic school uniform, fooling around with friends. A thirtyish executive type, really built, stockings and high heels, nice breasts pushing against a white fitted shirt. Skinny, plump, trashy, brainy—whatever. It didn't take much for me to become infatuated back then. Just a normal young libido and a healthy imagination. That was a time long past, so why did I find myself wondering if Ms. Paxinou would ever play Keely Smith to my Louis Prima?

"Ray Lawson," she said, "so good to see you. Are you here to celebrate the ICI or just to party?"

"I'm actually here to see what I can dig up on NoLab, but no luck tonight. I was just thinking about heading out, but now that you're here…"

"Yes, Carter told me you were looking for NoLab. Well, I've been here way too long myself. Perhaps I can contribute a little information to your investigation. Would you be interested in going somewhere to chat?"

"Absolutely. I'd love to. Besides, I'm starving. Can't ever seem to eat at these events."

I was about to learn a lot about Carter Wilkinson, the Institute, NoLab, and the transcendent Ms. Paxinou. Her first name is Allana.

If you like to go unnoticed, forget walking down the street or sitting in a restaurant with Allana. With her pure white hair, her blue-green eyes, and her regal bearing, people literally stop and stare.

We grabbed a booth in the least trendy joint we could find.

"You know, the day you and Victor were at the Institute was officially my last day of work there. Now I'm a curator at the Luce Center. I'm so much happier."

"The Luce Center, well that makes sense."

"If you know the Luce you're a rare man. To most, even in the art world, it might just as well be in the Sudan."

"Well, I love its concept. It's close to my heart. It displays *all* the artifacts in the collection, not just the best. The objects in unison create a truer history and seem to stand against elitist notions like quality."

"You really do know the Luce, Ray. I'm impressed. If you ever want to do P.R. for us, just let me know." She fidgeted with her cell phone and said, "I'm so glad we bumped into each other."

I recalled an image I'd seen long ago in Florence, Italy—the Parmigianino painting, *Madonna with the Long Neck*. The Madonna's right hand is the painting's focal point, graceful elongated fingers rest lightly on her chest, just above her breast. Until Allana was born, hands like that only existed in art.

"When you were at the Institute I wanted to talk to you, but I couldn't of course. Now I can, though there are still many things I can't discuss because of my non-disclosure agreement," said Allana.

I ordered fish and chips. Allana's a vegetarian, but I was impressed with how much Guinness she downed. She revealed many interesting things that night. According to Allana, the Foundation arm of the Institute supports some smart and worthwhile projects. It pumped a lot of cash into the defunct, online *Journal of Mundane Behavior*. So now the *JMB* is up and running again as a glossy print publication. In addition to academics, they can now afford celebrity contributors like Nicholson Baker, and this April they devoted an entire issue to *The Mezzanine*.

Allana said, "The Foundation arm also supports some extreme art projects."

"Would you include NoLab in that category?"

"Yes."

"But the folder the Institute gave us was so innocuous..."

"Ray, don't be so naïve. The Institute would never put anything in print that could be incriminating. I do know that NoLab spent a lot of the time in the Institute computer lab."

"I hear you. What kind of computer technology does it have?"

"My guess is it's up there with Langley—on a greatly reduced scale of course."

"I'd sure love knowing what they did in that lab."

"You should speak to Dr. Breedlove, the Research Director at the Institute. Perhaps she could answer some of your questions."

Allana couldn't say much more, but her final revelation was, to me, the most unsettling. She was clearly uncomfortable and spoke hesitatingly, "When I was at the Institute I was introduced to six other employees. We became the constituents of a group unofficially known as Chrome Club. Every club member possessed a rare genetic syndrome, no two the same. It was pretty clear that we were hired, at least in part, to satisfy Carter's need to possess rare and exotic things. I have Hagen-Griffiths syndrome." After rolling her napkin into a small tube, she said, "It's late, I've got to go. When you get home, Google Hagen-Griffiths."

"I'll do that, Allana."

So, Chrome Club was another Carter Wilkinson collection. Victor was right, something's not quite right about Wilkinson. Assembling a group of human beings with genetic abnormalities is definitely on the kinky side. Allana and I exchanged numbers and email addresses and agreed to meet again soon.

***

Hagen-Griffiths Syndrome

From the *Fleisher Index of Genetic and Rare Diseases*, 12 ed., 2014

Physiology: Individuals with Hagen-Griffiths syndrome have intense viridian irises and straight, pure white hair. The hands of those affected appear extremely graceful. Every finger contains an extra phalanx. Typically, there is narrowing of the aorta producing supravalvular aortic stenosis (SVAS), or narrowing of the pulmonary arteries

Cognition: Hagen-Griffiths children develop verbal language skills quite early, displaying a predilection for language that rhymes. They have difficulty writing print (geometric) letters but excel at cursive writing. At all developmental levels, they score well above average on standard I.Q. tests.

History: Hagen-Griffiths syndrome was first identified in 1958 by Dr. Louis Hagen in Toronto. In 1981 the genetic defect that causes H-G syndrome was discovered by a team of researchers led by Dr. S. Griffiths at the University of California, Berkeley. Caused by a mutation of genetic material in chromosome 7, H-G syndrome is extremely rare, occurring in 1 of every 1,250,000 births.

6

My phone woke me up. "Hello, Victor. You Okay?"

"Yeah, yeah. I just had a thought about NoLab."

"What? At five a.m.! Can't it wait?"

"Well, I can't sleep…"

"Jeez, Victor. I was up late last night. So, what is it?"

"It's this dream, a nightmare really."

"You're calling me because you had a bad dream. What are you, four years old? And why are you whispering?"

"I don't want to wake Savitha."

"I think I'm gonna hang up."

"No, just listen. You know I'm no touchy-feely kind of guy, but this dream was incredibly real. It was so fucking spooky, Ray. It really got to me, got to my core. And…I think it may be telling us something about NoLab."

"I really can't believe I'm hearing you say these words."

"Just listen. I was in a sleazy hotel, standing in the center of a dark room. Dave, our Dave, was on a couch making love, now get this: he was making love to a chimpanzee, yes, a *chimp-pan-zee*, and I do I mean *making love*, not fucking. It was mutual, romantic lovemaking. I heard Dave talking and heard their squeaks, gurgles, moans, and yelps. It was tender, warm, and wet. Then, abruptly, I was in a suburban ranch house. You know how dreams jerk you around in space and time."

"Yes, yes, go on."

"Well, Kaylee and Dave were there, sitting at a table, eating apples, and there were big red, yellow, and blue plastic toys scattered around, and a kid's swing set. Then a young monkey or chimp-like thing appears. It's crying and squealing and wearing a diaper. It runs across the room, jumps in Dave's arms, and says—'DADA'. No other dream ever got to me quite like this...and, you know, of course, it reminded me of Dave's obsession in grad school. Remember?"

"Yeah, sure. Monkeys."

"Simians. He knew *everything* on the subject. Everything!"

"So, Victor, are you trying to tell me you think NoLab is hiding out somewhere trying to create a human-chimp hybrid? Is that what you're saying?"

"Yes. A humanzee!"

"And you think this because you had a dream?"

"I know it's crazy, but it would be the perfect NoLab act: transgressive, creative, paradigm-shifting," said Victor.

"Creepy." I said, "Besides, you know, it's pretty much impossible. The biggest, most advanced science labs in the world can't do shit like that, so there's sure as hell no way NoLab can. Your idea is ridiculous, but I give you an A for creativity."

"Ray, scientists can't do it because they can't go there, it's taboo. Verboten. It would forever change how human beings view themselves and their relationship to animals."

"You're getting carried away, as usual, but sure, it would create a million new problems the world doesn't need right now. How would humanzees be treated? They'd probably be exploited and abused. Would they simply become hairy humans with full rights? I really doubt it. More likely to end up as slave labor, designer pets, or caged amusements."

"With Pinky's or Wilkinson's money and with NoLab's academic connections they could definitely put together a team of biologists that could take a good stab at a transgenic interspecies creation. This really has all the earmarks of a NoLab project."

"Whatever. Thanks for the wake-up call. Don't forget, in just a few hours, we're leaving for the Island."

"I'll be ready," whispered Victor.

***

Victor was right on time. He arrived 9 a.m. at my loft an Avenue A. We headed north toward the Queens Midtown Tunnel. Destination: the Long Island home of Woody Redman, cyber sleuth. As we approached 12th Street, a large S.U.V. darted out of a curbside parking space and hit us, gently, but with enough momentum to dent the sheet metal and scratch the paint on the right rear fender of our little Ford Fiesta. Victor enjoyed calling it a Ford Fiasco. Victor got out of the car, as did the driver of the offending vehicle, a big jolly man wearing a pink alligator-shirt and khaki pants. Jolly's wife remained in the S.U.V. The man suggested they forget the whole incident, no need to exchange insurance information, as the damage was so slight. He concluded by saying, "After all, we're both good Christians, aren't we?" Victor, abruptly, and with a dead-cold severity I'd never seen before, looked into Jolly's eyes and replied, "Like fuck we are." The two exchanged license and insurance information and we went on our way without discussing the incident.

I told Victor about my dinner with Allana, described her new position at the Luce, and all the amazing things the foundation arm of Carter Wilkinson's Institute was up to. Victor was impressed; I knew he would be, but when I told him about Chrome Club he went ballistic.

"Wilkinson's a goddamned psycho! Sounds like a page out of Dr. Mengele's journal. What's he gonna do, start breeding humans? And...Ray, my dream is looming larger—doesn't Wilkinson seem like a guy who would like to create a humanzee? Doesn't he? The Institute is definitely behind NoLab's vanishing act. That's it—next week—go after Wilkinson! Let's get inside the Institute and look around, but this time uninvited."

I didn't respond. Something prevented me from being totally convinced that Wilkinson was our man, maybe I liked him too much. And, I didn't want to play SWAT team, which is, I'm certain, exactly what Victor had in mind. His plan, no doubt, was to break in and snoop around, dressed in black, wearing body armor and night vision goggles. The Institute was clearly a well-secured, high tech building. There was no way we could get in. Well, no way without Allana's assistance, and that just wasn't going to happen. I was hoping for a non-violent solution, like getting Woody to do all the breaking-in, virtually, that is.

***

My lawyer, Grace Germain, called once again about old Madison Clark. He wanted to meet to discuss his claims. I took out my anger on poor Germain. "My pill pieces were *vitamins* compared with the legal poison they push every day on television. Have you seen the lethal side effects of those drugs? Heart failure, liver failure, even death. Difficulty breathing, swelling of the face, tongue, throat. Hallucinations, panic attacks, depression, suicidal thoughts. And shit like that for ailments as ridiculous as restless-leg syndrome and acne..."

"Ray, Ray, Ray—relax, this isn't a real case. Let's just meet him, humor him. It'll be fine."

We set up a few available dates for the meeting.

***

Woody was an amazing resource. He did a lot of work for big law firms, Homeland Security, and the NSA. Obviously, people like Woody are increasingly valuable in today's world, and obviously what we've been asking him to do for us was far below his level of expertise. The information that Woody was retrieving for us was peanuts, but Woody was a friend and besides, he knew NoLab. In fact, he and Dave had spent countless hours together at CASTL, Columbia's Computer Architecture and Security Technologies Lab. Woody and Dave were the rare art students who rose out of computer graphics to the darker mysteries of programming. Dave was an able hacker; Woody was a master.

After obtaining an MS in Computer Science from Stanford, Woody returned to Valley Stream to live in his parents' home. The greater his withdrawal from the world, the more profound his obsession with numbers, data, and networks. In the avocado -colored bedroom of his childhood—with Claire and Charlie, his mom and dad, just down the hall—Woody did his thing. When Victor and I visited him, Claire insisted we stay for dinner. The chrome and Formica table, the plastic plates, and tall glasses with multicolor stripes were, I'm certain, all obtained when Claire and Charlie Redman first moved into the little ranch house on Willow Lane. Good, frugal people; decent, honest people. The Redmans didn't ask for much; they were content with what they had. Little did they know what shadowy, Byzantine activities took place in the confines of Woody's bedroom.

Dinner was color-coordinated—salmon croquettes, creamed corn, mashed potatoes. The subtle differences between these warm, low intensity, close-valued hues would have pleased Albers. Dessert: butterscotch pudding. Haven't had this kind of food since Perry Como sang "find a wheel." Time stood still in every room, except Woody's. There he spent his days and nights navigating infinitely branching labyrinths. Woody worked with classified information and tracked ISIS funding patterns, his depression deepening.

Woody didn't say much at dinner. Claire talked about Woody's childhood.

"Woodruff was a big chubby baby, but look at him now. You're too thin, you've got to eat, Woody."

Charlie told us all about the chain mail armor he was making for the upcoming Medieval Reenactment Games at Roosevelt Field. He was really into it. Charlie was an insurance rep, and Claire a secretary at Nassau Community College. Not a mean bone in their bodies. The world would do well to have a lot more like Claire and Charlie Redman. When we departed, they insisted that we take doggie bags.

***

Information on Carter Wilkinson, as provided by Woody Redman:

In 1999 Wilkinson received a B.A. in Philosophy from Princeton. In 2002 he was the recipient of a Ph.D. in Mathematics from M.I.T. While still in graduate school, and when he wasn't at the Mohegan Sun blackjack tables, Wilkinson began to obtain corporate consulting contracts. This work quickly revealed a very special talent—zero-gravity thinking. ZG thinkers are experts in their disciplines but not expert in the disciplines of the institutions that invite them to consult.

In 2000, Wilkinson, along with about a dozen others, was a zero-gravity thinker in the experimental unit AIZG, the artificial intelligence division of DARPA and its private sector partner, Sentient Eye. This was just one of thousands of attempts over many decades by numerous research teams to develop computers that can learn on their own and interact seamlessly with humans. Passing the Turing Test was the big prize. Everyone was seeking computers that could author and understand jokes, for example. DARPA and Sentient have brilliant engineers, but A.I. is obviously not an engineering problem. Good zero-gravity thinkers can often solve the unsolvable by seeing big patterns. They aren't afraid to ask dumb questions, and they aren't weighed down by ingrained disciplinary methodologies and stifling corporate cultures.

While the contents of Wilkinson's recommendation have never been made public, his report remains legendary in A.I. circles and is rumored to have focused on the philosophy of consciousness and the perception of pleasure and pain. Sentient took Wilkinson's ideas and ran with them. Wilkinson, in exchange for a sweet royalty deal, handed Sentient Eye the Holy Grail.

Carter Wilkinson began parlaying his Sentient royalties and investment profits into shorting the housing bubble at the peak of the real estate boom. In 2007 his hedge fund, Wilkinson, Teal & Magnus, made thirteen billion on credit default swaps on securitized mortgage debt when the subprime crisis hit. He became one of the world's fifty richest people but always managed to stay out of the media and under the radar.

7

Woody informed us that Dr. Crystal Breedlove, the Institute's research director, was to be speaking at the College Art Society conference in Los Angeles. Since Allana believed Breedlove could have some answers for us, Victor and I decided to catch a flight to L.A. to meet her. We arrived at the Millennium Biltmore pretty late. Wound down with dirty martinis. The next morning we registered for the conference and picked up our packets. Over bad coffee in the hotel restaurant, Victor told me he didn't get much sleep, too revved up. "There was a car chase on channel five. Ray, it was mesmerizing. Can't say why exactly. Everyone knows the guy's gonna get caught in the end. The cops tried to pull over this frigging maniac in an old Buick for some minor traffic infraction. Instead of stopping, the guy took off. It made no sense. The Buick guy just floored it and got on 101. He's on it forever, getting up to a hundred miles an hour. About six police cars are tailing him. A police helicopter is hovering overhead with a spotlight on the car. It's a circus. What can he be thinking? He got on the 405, off at Wilshire Boulevard, then he's on surface streets and gunning it through intersections. Eventually, he makes a wide turn, too wide, and hit a parked car. Hit pretty hard. So then, this very intelligent individual got out of the car and ran for it. Of course, the whole thing's being broadcast from a helicopter. There's nowhere he can go. The crazy chase went on for an hour, and the good folks at KTLA aired it all—screw whatever else was supposed to be on then, I guess. Never saw anything quite like this back east. Well, that's why I didn't get much sleep, too revved up."

Victor's got the enthusiasm. Good for him.

We finished our coffee and checked out the schedule.

"These profs are comic geniuses," said Victor. "Chris Rock, eat your heart out." I guess you would have to say that Victor and I are bad academics. We're those tenured radicals who frighten conservatives. Victor read his favorite lecture titles from the session listings:

-The Burden of Authenticity: Strategies for Retaining Indexical Origins in the Conservation of Seventeenth-Century Indo-Portuguese Ivory Statuettes

-Illusory Materiality: Toward a Reconsideration of Francesco Furini's Multi-Composite Facture

-Statistical Methodologies for Exploring Cross-Cultural Hybridization in the Mattamayura Saiva Monastic Architecture in Early Medieval Central India

"So amazing," Victor said. "It would be great if these were spoofs, but sadly, they're sincere."

"Victor, you know your eyes look kind of weird."

"Weird how?"

"Turn this way, let me see." He looked older, still kind of handsome, but haggard. "The whites of your eyes are definitely yellowish," I said.

"Ah, that's just age. Got those spots popping up on my hands, my hair is thinning, skin sagging, so I'm not surprised that my eyes are changing too. You know, Ray, I can actually feel the last fucking drops of testosterone ebbing from my body and—this may be crazy, but I like it. Fewer diversions. Fewer anger management problems, fewer driving incidents, the middle finger is displayed less frequently. I almost feel like what I imagine normal people must feel like, less hostile, more considerate—happy. Testosterone isn't a Neapolitan dessert, it's a dangerous drug."

"That's funny, Victor, but your eyes are definitely yellow. Jaundice is a symptom of some serious shit. You should see your doctor."

"Okay, boss, don't worry. Will do."

We found Crystal Breedlove in the schedule. Her session was coming up at noon. Perfect. We got to the concourse meeting room 408B early enough to introduce ourselves. Arranged a time to meet for dinner that evening—she suggested a new restaurant in Culver City. She wrote its name, Taxi, and its address on the back of her card. We sat through one other lecture before Breedlove gave her talk, *The Misfits: The Replacement of Art by Popular Culture, Mass Media, and Technology.*

Dr. Breedlove was introduced, the lights dimmed and an

image of Clark Gable roping a wild horse appeared on the screen behind her. She began.

The 1961 movie, The Misfits, *written by Arthur Miller and directed by John Huston, serves as a metaphor for the predicament faced by contemporary artists. It explores the struggle to maintain traditions in a changing world, the impact of technology, and the myth of the American cowboy.*

In The Misfits, *Clark Gable and Montgomery Clift play cowboys in 1950s Nevada. They round up wild mustangs for a living. Marilyn Monroe, as a recent divorce', shows up and promptly falls in love with Gable. All goes well until she finds out that the horses they are catching are being sold for dog food, not for riding, as they once were. Monroe, the conscience of the movie, fights to put an end to the tainted enterprise, but Gable and Clift defend their lifestyle.*

Though Gable insists they are doing the same thing they always did, it is a blatant falsehood. They pursue wild mustangs while riding in the back of a truck and lasso each horse with a rope attached to a tire that is thrown off the truck. The mustangs pull the tires around in the desert until exhausted, ready for easy pickup.

Like this cowboy tale, postmodernity is marked by a loss of faith in existing constructs. We are caught up in a world whose belief systems are coming undone. Confusion reigns as art's foundation erodes. The crisis of confidence in the art community is part of the larger malaise. As Gable's character finally discovered, maintaining a lifestyle and an ethic in a shifted landscape cannot be achieved by an allegiance to pre-existing forms and conventions.

After a dramatic scene in which Gable single-handedly recaptures a horse released by Clift and Monroe after a roundup, Gable's character says: "Damn it all. They changed it all around. Smeared it all over with blood. I'm finished with it. It's like ropin' a dream now. Gotta find another way to be alive, that's all, if there is one, anymore."

Like those who support the spirit of the law as opposed to the letter, we must engage the spirit of art, not its material form nor its emptied conventions. The spirit of art is alive and well in our culture—how could it be otherwise? It is just not where those of us in the arts want it to be.

The spirit of art now forms a tremendously rich and complex culture which is a veritable extravaganza of esthetic and transformative events that surround us everywhere, from the automobile showroom to your Facebook page, from the local mall to the apps on your iPhone—these are the true inheritors of the spirit of Lascaux, the Sistine Chapel, and the modern studio as places for the creation of fantasy, magic, beauty, information, commentary, subversion.

If you want to observe the phenomena that are transforming our world, don't look at Artforum; look at the business section of The New York Times; if you want to see amazing displays of color, shape, and texture juxtaposed with intelligence and abandon, don't look at Art in America, look at Vogue. Fashion magazines are, pound for pound, the best inventories of sheer visual pleasure. Artists have long since abandoned exploring this territory with any conviction.

Projected text:

"I love my automobile…she is my life, my artistic and spiritual life…full of riches…she is more dear, more useful, more full of education than my library, where the closed books sleep on their

spines, than my paintings, which hang dead on my walls all around me, with their immobile sky, tree, water, and figures..."
         - Octave Mirbeau, 1908

Roland Barthes called the modern automobile "the exact equivalent of the great Gothic cathedrals: I mean the supreme creation of an era, conceived with passion by unknown artists, and consumed in image if not in usage by a whole population which appropriates them as a purely magical object."

A handful of mumbling attendees exited the auditorium and Victor looked at me and said, "The truth of it is, Dr. Breedlove could be shot for this. She's coming off like some kind of anarchist, not exactly what the professional art idolaters want to hear."

New modes of communication outside the realm of fine art have usurped the traditional roles of art. These new forms have forced contemporary artists to reconstruct ersatz historical models or to develop novelties, searching for a place, a purpose, and an identity that is not already occupied by other cultural practices. It is all too clear that the project of art has become the project of saving art. Art is left the self-conscious task of attempting profundity, jockeying for a spot next to Pollock in the Museum of Modern Art. Philip Fisher calls artifacts produced after the advent of the museum, "cunning objects...objects that have as their single, overt design, the desire to join history...."

By the end of Breedlove's talk there were many empty seats.

She entertained questions and received only a few.

The first query was a blunt and angry one—the woman rose and asked, "Why do you hate art?"

Breedlove replied, "If you think that's the essential idea of this talk, then either I failed miserably or you weren't listening. No, I certainly do not hate art. I love art. I studied Early Netherlandish painting at Barnard. I shouldn't have to be saying this, nor should I have to summarize the half-hour lecture that I just delivered. I simply suggested that serious attention be paid to the vitality of the wide cultural universe outside of the art world."

The questioner remained standing and said, "I still think you hate art."

The second question, from a gray-haired man sporting a ponytail, "What are the core competencies of your new pop culture art practice?"

As poor Breedlove struggled to answer, Victor leaned toward me and said, "If you ever hear me say the words 'core competencies,' please shoot me between the fucking eyes."

***

Back in the depressing Millennium Biltmore bar, Victor went into molto mode.

"Ray, did you ever watch *Have Gun—Will Travel* when you were a kid?"

"Watch what?"

"*Have Gun—Will Travel*, a TV Western with Richard Boone."

"Uh, no, I don't think so."

"Do you know Richard Boone?"

"I guess not."

"He was an awesome, rugged dude—not your typical Hollywood pretty face. He played the part of Paladin. Each episode began with a gun pointed directly at the TV audience, with Boone's voice-over: 'I'd like you to take a look at this gun. The balance is excellent. The trigger responds to a pressure of one ounce. This gun was handcrafted to my specification and I rarely draw it unless I mean to use it.'"

"You memorized that?" I asked.

"Listen to me. This is important! All that talk about *The Misfits* was, like, my madeleine," said Victor.

"Okay."

"Listen up, Ray. Paladin lived the life of a San Francisco gentleman, stayed at the chichi Hotel Carlton, wore a four-button suit jacket, satin vest, and frilly white shirt. He appreciated fine food and good wine, knew a lot about art, literature, and history. He charmed women with his courtly manners, *but*—he was a loner—no buddies, no family. Paladin is a hired gun. His calling card bears an image of a chess knight and reads: 'Have Gun Will Travel—Wire Paladin—San Francisco.' Dressed in black from hat to boot, he rode alone for days in rugged terrain to defend decent people from ruthless outlaws. He always prevailed."

"Are you crying, Victor?"

"Hey, these are happy tears. You know…Paladin had a lot to do with what I thought an artist should be and how life should be lived. Paladin was every inch an artist (and not just because he dressed in black). While maintaining a disregard for money, he enjoyed the pleasure and the power it afforded, and like many artists, he succeeded in living in two worlds simultaneously. In one he was a connoisseur of luxury and refinement, a man of leisure and erudition—free of institutional responsibility. In the other, he lived a life of physical action—danger and the celebration of strength, and skill. Periodically he rode off on his lonely missions. That's us in the studio, Ray! Are you with me?"

"Yeah, yeah, go on, I like it. Do you want another Moretti?"

Victor nodded, yes, and continued his tribute.

"Like all true artists, Paladin was self-employed, worked alone (for deserving clients only), and always did things his way. His color-blind commitment to fair play, his willingness to risk his life for the rights of the defenseless, and his insistence on social justice made a huge impression on me."

"Sounds religious," I said.

"Yes, the show was a weekly sermon. These simple stories, in black and white, on funky, little round-cornered TV screens, interrupted by the most ridiculous commercials, were as gloriously mythological as the tales of John Henry, as humanistic as Zen parables, and as pure and spare as Shaker furniture."

"Amen, brother, amen."

NoLab

***

Breedlove's ideas were not unlike scores of twentieth-century avant-garde artists and theorists who believed in leveling the cultural playing field. In fact, hasn't this been the dominant trajectory of all contemporary culture? Marsden Hartley said, "Reduce the size of the 'A' in art, to meet the size of the rest of the letters in one's speech." Kaprow said, "Nonart is more art than Art art." Cultural anthropologists taught us to value *every* cultural manifestation, from courting rituals to cooking, not just "high" culture—this insight did far more to alter the course of art than the camera and all the technologies ever developed. If you want to understand contemporary culture, you're better off visiting a monster truck show or an Apple store than an art museum or symphony performance. Breedlove, however, had a way of making it all sound threatening and apocalyptic, but that didn't deter Victor and me from our ideological attraction to her position, and so I suppose to the ideas of the goddamned Institute itself, putting us in the conflicted position of camaraderie with the very institution we suspected of malevolence.

Later that night Victor and I found our way to the Santa Monica Freeway and headed west to meet Breedlove at Taxi. As usual, there was heavy traffic. *Tengo Que Colgar*, the song on the radio, was followed by a jingle for a restaurant called Meshuga 4 Sushi and a warning about an ostrich causing traffic problems— I didn't catch the location. Victor usually dressed well, casually, inconspicuously, but this evening he wore a black t-shirt with white text on the front: 'Too Dumb for New York, Too Ugly for L.A.'

I said, "Was the shirt really necessary?"

"I guess that means you don't like it."

"It's stupid."

"Ray, I have the feeling we are being tailed," said Victor.

"Who is it?"

"Don't know. It's just a feeling. I noticed a car acting funny, but it's more like something I am just…sensing. Anyhow, just keep an eye out, okay?"

Tailed, I like that word, don't think anyone has ever said that to me before. Just a movie word. Victor's got extrasensory perception, thinks he's some kind of Comanche scout. "Okay, I'll pay attention," I said.

Later, at our exit, we were cut off by a pickup truck with a blaring horn and a bumper sticker that read, "If you don't like my driving dial 1-800-EAT-SHIT." Victor said, "That pretty much sums up America today, don't ya think?"

We made our way to our destination on Overland. Taxi was jumping, lots of young lovelies at the bar. From the look of things, you'd never know the economy was hurting. Breedlove was already there. Rolling her eyes, she said to Victor, "Nice shirt."

Victor said, "Thanks."

As Breedlove and I air-kissed, I said, "Good to see you, Crystal."

At the table, I asked, "So, what's good to order at Taxi?"

"Taxi, what's that?" she responded.

"Uh, Taxi, isn't this Taxi?" I said. Still no response. Victor held up the menu, and pointed—"Taxi, see."

"Oh sorry, yes, Taxi," she said, laughing.

"Okay, what's the joke?" asked Victor.

"No joke, gentleman, sorry, but the restaurant's name is pronounced *fosado*."

"Well, how's that?" said Victor. "There's no earthly connection between those two words, it's ridiculous."

"Well, ridiculous it may be, but *everyone* knows the name of this restaurant is pronounced fosado, it's fosado, that's just the way it is."

Victor asked, "How do you spell fosado?"

"Here in Culver City it's spelled T-A-X-I."

"I know Oaxaca (he pronounced it ow-acksika) is pronounced wahaka, and quinoa (kwin-oh-ah) is keenwah, but, sorry, there's just no way Taxi can be fosado," Victor said.

"Perhaps this place is a branch of the Museum of Jurassic Technology," I said.

"No, this name game is just an ugly device that separates the uninformed slobs of the world from the hip, up to the minute, beautiful people. I don't find that kind of exclusionary wordplay amusing," said Victor.

"Hey guys, chill!" said Breedlove. "Let's order. It's on Carter, you know, the Institute."

"Yes, let's order. I'll be having a martini, and by the way, that's spelled E-A-T-M-E," said Victor.

"Victor, you know I don't own this restaurant, right?" said Breedlove. "It's not *my* restaurant. I didn't name this restaurant. And besides, artists aren't the only ones who can play with conventions, so let the little people have some fun."

"Hmm." After a long pause, Victor said, "Yeah…you're right Crystal, sorry. After all these years I'm still working on my anger management problem."

The waitress arrived and introduced herself. "Hi, my name is Celebrity Holmes and I'll be your server tonight." When the cocktails and little plates arrived we all laughed and toasted loony L.A. Victor said, "Ray and I *really* liked your talk, but your audience is invested in an archaic idea of art. Why do you bother?"

"Thank you, Victor—you may be right about my audience, but you guys teach, and most of your students probably have pretty conservative views."

"Yes, but students are more malleable than your crowd today—those art historians are dug in deep—and anyway, at this point, *we* attract the crazies," I said.

"Right, and we really don't *teach* teach, we just engage the Infinite Monkey Theorem," said Victor.

"Uh huh, what's that?"

"I'm sure you've heard of it. It goes something like: Given enough time or an infinite amount of time, a monkey randomly striking keys on a typewriter will end up writing *Hamlet*. Sometimes it's described as an infinite number of monkeys typing."

"Oh yes, I've heard of that," said Crystal.

"Well, we just put a lot of grad students in studios, and every ten years or so one will stumble upon something extraordinary," said Victor.

"I did the talk because Carter asked me to. He thought it would be good for the Institute to finally poke its head out of the burrow. But, it wasn't as much fun as I expected it to be."

"Tell us about Carter," I said.

"Carter. Well, he's larger than life, quite brilliant and as you know, spectacularly wealthy. Deep thoughts and deep pockets. You've been to the Institute, so you know he's a man possessed. He's gathered an amazing group of curators and advisors. I'm proud to be on the team and I believe in the mission."

"What do you make of Chrome Club?" I asked.

"Wow, that's a tough one, hmm…well, I wish *I* had some *superpowers*." She laughed, paused for a while, and said, "Then I might get invited to join the club. But really, Chrome Club doesn't seem to be a big deal. It's not a joke, but, also, as a unit, it doesn't participate in the operations of the Institute. I guess I think it's just a little something for Carter Wilkinson's amusement. Personally, I don't really get it."

"It creeps me out," said Victor.

"Victor, Victor, relax! There's really no need to be *creeped out*." As Crystal pronounced the words creeped out, she made air quotes around them. "You seem to think Carter is some kind of weirdo. Well, he *is* unusual, but that's all. In fact, I think he's actually quite saintly. Who else would fund the Brown and Beige Society? He devoted a lot of time to this little outfit. Just so you know how I see it—Carter's a humanist," said Crystal.

"The Brown and *what* Society?" said Victor.

"The Brown and Beige Society. It's a group of young linguists trying to change the world by changing language. The name of the group is a good example of what they're up to. You know how we say black and white to describe racial difference? Well those designations are polar opposites, extreme dichotomies, when in reality, skin color ranges mostly between beige and brown."

"Yeah, similar to the range of color in wood," I said.

"Right. In other words, we're more alike than different. These linguists believe inaccurate language increases the racial divide," said Crystal.

"I like the idea of these Brown and Beigers, I really do. Though, it doesn't mean Carter's a saint," said Victor.

"Are you enjoying your oysters?" Crystal asked.

"Divine darling," said Victor, affectedly.

"They make a fine collection," said Crystal. "Kumamotos, Humboldt Golds, and Malpeques. People don't see the curating and collecting that surrounds them. Almost everything is curated, every item on a menu, the carefully chosen furniture in your living room, the people you invite to a dinner party, the clothing in your closet, the socks in your drawer—collections are everywhere and we're all curators!"

"Well said," I responded.

"Thanks, but I didn't say things well enough this afternoon to avoid the fang marks on my neck."

Victor had a dreamy look in his eyes. He said, "Collections are bundles of nouns. No verbs, no adjectives, no ornament. It seems we all agree on the power and importance of collections."

"Almost blood brothers," said Crystal as she reached toward Victor. They grasped hands across the table in what looked like a heartfelt homie handshake.

Victor continued. "Years ago I saw this pretty ridiculous movie, I think it was called *Throw Mama from the Train*,"—Crystal's eyebrows lifted—"Don't laugh my hipster friend! Please stay with me. One scene was quite touching. The character played by Danny DeVito asked the Billy Crystal character if he wanted to see his coin collection."

"Nice name," said Crystal.

"Yes! I actually missed that. Well, *this* Crystal was totally uninterested in seeing the collection, but DeVito spread the coins out anyway. They were just ordinary quarters, nickels, and pennies, neither valuable nor rare—astonishingly unexceptional—until DeVito told the story behind each one. One was change from a Peter, Paul, and Mary concert his father took him to, another—change his dad let him keep from a hot dog purchased at the circus. This pitiful six-coin collection from DeVito's childhood was *change that his father let him keep*. Pretty saccharine stuff, but I had a good cry."

"That story does a great job of suggesting a humanistic alternative to our current value system," said Crystal. "Sorry I rolled my eyes—I too saw a sentimental movie about love and collecting. I sobbed at the end of *Cinema Paradiso*. When the old projectionist died he bequeathed a film reel to his young apprentice, now a grown man and a famous film director. Remember? They were bound by their love of cinema. The reel was a montage of all the kissing scenes cut from the films before they were shown—the sexy parts that were censored by the village priest. Wow."

"Wow indeed! Saw that movie long ago, so beautiful," I said. "Okay then, how about *Smoke*?"

"Ah, *Smoke*. A photograph every day, same time, same place. What was the great line?" said Crystal.

"'Slow down my friend,'" I said.

"Yes, there was a whole world in that seemingly boring photo collection," said Crystal.

"Yes! *Smoke*," said Victor.

Celebrity Holmes arrived with our espressos.

"Can I ask you about NoLab, Crystal? Did you know them or work with them?"

"Carter warned me that you would be asking."

"Did he tell you what to say?" asked Victor.

"Anger management problems and paranoia too. That must make life difficult."

"Yes, it's a daily struggle," said Victor, feigning despair.

"Well, I never met any of the NoLab members, but I do know they were the recipients of a small project grant or two. Some kind of research involving the financial aspects of the art world. Carter really likes NoLab. They even mingled socially on occasion, which was quite unusual—Carter basically keeps to himself. Hey, that's pretty much all I know," Crystal said.

Breedlove was smart and sassy, couldn't help liking her. Our goal of finding NoLab, however, seemed increasingly unattainable. The following day, we returned to New York.

8

It may not have been the best moment to attend a show at MASS MoCA, but Victor and I definitely needed some R & R. Since the NoLab search was at an impasse we decided to clear our heads in North Adams, Massachusetts. The event was an opening for an old friend, Sydney Bower. We decided to make the long drive. Victor took the opportunity to get to see Corey—he arranged for Savitha, his latest female friend, to chaperon Corey on Amtrak to MASS MoCA for the opening. Corey loved trains and parties—Savitha did too.

During the drive to North Adams, Victor sat silently. It was just not like Victor. I could see he was in pain. He said he'd be fine, lunch didn't agree with him, just needed to rest. When we arrived at the hotel, he required assistance getting out of the car. Something was obviously wrong. He went straight to his room.

Four hours later, Victor knocked on my door. As he entered, I said, "Greetings, sir. Feeling okay now?"

"Yes, I slept the entire time. That was what I needed, some rest." The T.V. was on—CNN was broadcasting a Trump campaign speech. Victor began running around the room, his ears covered by his hands, yelling, "Fuck, fuck, turn it off, fuck,

fuck, fuck…" Excellent! Victor was feeling better.

In the evening, at the exhibition opening, Victor seemed just fine—like nothing happened. Savitha arrived, Corey in tow. Victor was clearly thrilled to see them both. The event was quite grand. Since there were three exhibitions opening that evening, many art world luminaries attended. Thelma Golden, Donna De Salvo, Tino Sehgal, James Turrell, Katharina Grosse, Roberta Smith, Jerry Saltz, Tom Eccles, and Anne Pasternak. Breedlove and lots of others were there as well, but Victor's posture improved markedly when Allana arrived. Distinguished guests aside, Corey, with his infectious enthusiasm, was the big hit. When he was asked if he thought a massive, black Richard Serra drawing was art, he replied, "not yet." As the speechmaking began, Allana and Corey wandered off hand in hand, chattering and laughing. Victor and Savitha headed to the bar.

Sydney's installation, *Web Life*, consisted of a live-stream video projection. The subject, an actual living spider in its web, high up and out of sight on a ledge in the northwest corner of the space. The spider's micro-engineering feat was projected real-time on the huge south wall in super-high resolution, enormously enlarged, using state of the art equipment.

Delicate and poetic slammed up against massive and threatening. A commonplace little event became a spectacle of the sublime. A hidden, mundane occurrence was pulled from the margins and celebrated. I think it was Al Held who said, "Conceptual art is just pointing at things." Well, Sydney's little Bodhi-cam pointed most eloquently.

The noise level in the hall rose from a murmur to a roar. Everyone headed to the room that housed Sydney's installation. My natural instinct was to go in the opposite direction, but not to embarrass myself in front of Allana I followed the crowd. Cocktails in hand, dressed to the nines, all were drawn to the spider web projection. A tiny moth had drifted into the web. People were gasping, saying "Oh no," "Jesus," "Oh my God." I must admit, their ridiculous overreactions seemed, somehow, appropriate; the violent struggle of this tiny speck of moth, massively projected, was painful to experience. The more it thrashed, the more ensnared it became. Some were calling for Sydney to rescue it, some for MASS MoCA to do something, others were laughing, saying things like, "Get a life, it's just a moth." It was a dramatic ending to the evening. Sydney could not have hoped for more.

During the drive back home to New York, I told Victor I had an upcoming dinner date with Allana. He said, "Ray, she is the one—capeesh?"

"Capeesh."

***

Allana's apartment was on the Upper East Side, kind of traditional, but spare. Not the kind of spare I've always aspired to, but uncluttered and unpretentious. In London, many years ago, I read about a then-new, East Asian restaurant, Wagamama. As I recall, one reviewer liked the food but complained about the décor, likened it to a "Swiss venereal disease clinic." Yes! That describes my ideal *machine for living*—severe, no decoration, stainless steel, right angles, antiseptic—yes, a Swiss venereal disease clinic! Unfortunately, my loft is a total mess—it's unbearable. At least I have my paintings. There alone can I maintain the desired degree of reductive rigor.

I was surprised to learn that Allana had a dog. Not many people I know have dogs. Too much trouble in the city, and picking up poop is a deal breaker for this pilgrim. It *was*, however, a pretty sweet dog—a mellow, mixed-breed rescue dog that just seemed to want affection. His name was Becher. I would have petted him more but I didn't want to get hair all over me.

While Allana made cocktails I checked out her photography collection. It was personal but not eccentric. All primo. Not the same old names everyone else collects. She really had some spectacular images: Chim's heartbreaking 1948 photo of a blind boy who lost his arms in World War II Italy—reading brail with his lips, the boy appears to be kissing the book; Winston O. Link's *Hotshot Eastbound,* and *Hester Fringer's living room on the tracks*; William Klein's photo of a *Vogue* model smoking, I think it's titled *Hat and Five Roses*; Pieter Hugo's hyena men; and some nice photos by Loretta Lux, Simen Johan, Weegee, the Bechers, and Camille Seaman, as well as three delightfully bonkers Martin Parr food pics. Considering Allana's history at the Institute and at the Luce, a photography collection made sense. Along with collections, archives, and lists, photography is an important player in the big documentary project, and the act of taking a photograph is just a sneaky way to steal the things you love. Refreshingly, the world is featured, not the artist. Egon Kisch said, "Nothing is more amazing than the simple truth, nothing is more exotic than our own surroundings, nothing is more fantastic in effect than objective description, and nothing is more remarkable than the time in which we live."

Allana came out of the kitchen with two tall glasses.

"Hope you like mojitos, Ray."

We talked about her photo collection, our backgrounds, families, and politics. She was easy to talk to, easy to be with.

Dinner was simple and elegant—asparagus, fennel, cacio e pepe and a nice Orvieto. Allana was eager to talk about her new project at the Luce. "The show I'm working on is about a category of realism that is largely overlooked, though quite widespread. It's the ultimate realism. It will consist of figurative, life-size, three-dimensional polychrome artifacts. Think fake plastic sushi on steroids. The artifacts in the show may belong to a marginalized category of representation, but the exhibition's gonna be a madcap romp. In addition to many beautiful works of actual sculpture, we'll have contemporary realism from the popular domain—plastic flowers, fruit, and food—also hunting decoys, fishing lures, toy guns—lots of toys, dolls, gag items, faux furs, wigs, prosthetic body parts, medical and scientific models, sex toys, knockoff handbags and fashion, and copies of classical sculpture. There'll be numerous examples in most every category, in true Luce fashion. Then the fun begins with the large items, cell towers that look like pine trees and cacti…we even obtained some wood and canvas tanks from WWII that were used as decoys, they're called dummy tanks.—I'm boring you."

"No, Allana. I'm fascinated. We're on the same wavelength here—totally. And besides, I'm happy just being with you."

"Well, I just realized I was rambling on. I'm excited about this show, started thinking about it for the Institute, where it would have been a more appropriate fit. Luckily the folks at the Luce are supporting it even though it diverges quite a bit from their mission. I think they just needed to do something sexy."

The conversation meandered from art to politics to food. Allana made a compelling case for vegetarianism. "Someday," she said, "the human race will stand disgraced by its bloody history. It will feel intense shame remembering the industrial-scale slaughter of all the harmless creatures, creatures with as much right to life as any human."

After dinner we continued talking; glasses of nocino warmed and relaxed us. Allana said, "I imagine you Googled my syndrome."

"Victor did. So, yes I do now know something about Hagen-Griffiths Syndrome, but even before reading about it, Victor and I sensed something special about you. In fact, I was mesmerized and—guess I should tell you, I still am." At that moment she leaned closer and put both hands over mine. She said, "Can you feel my extra phalanges?" I rubbed her fingers lightly and then massaged each joint and then her fingertips.

"As a child, I was so ashamed of my hands, my white hair, my eyes, the whole complex of syndrome characteristics. You know, kids just want to blend. I died my hair brown for years. Even today, sometimes I just want to disappear."

Still holding hands, I said, "No need to disappear, you are a genetic upgrade."

"You're kind, Ray, but I don't think I'll ever stop feeling like the mutant I am. I feel closer to Corey than I do to neurotypicals. You know, we're both genetic anomalies. He's got an extra twenty-first chromosome, and I have a mutated seventh. Unfortunately, Corey has no way to blend. I love that kid."

"What about the tendency to speak in rhyme? You clearly don't."

"Oh my God. I've been working on suppressing that little tic since I was twelve. It's a work in progress. Hope you never see me lose my temper, let down my guard—but if you do, you'll hear a lot rhyming."

"Since we're getting personal, can I ask you about Chrome Club? It makes Carter seem deranged, sinister even. If you don't want to go there, let's just drop it."

"No, I don't mind talking about it. Can't say I really understand it. I mean, it's not like we had meetings to discuss protecting Earth from invading space aliens, like some *X-Men* movie. I really don't know why Carter brought us all to the Institute. Maybe he doesn't know either. One of the preparators really thought Carter wanted to breed some kind of new race, but of course, there was no hint of anything like that, no directives of any kind, at least not when I was there. We didn't know about Chrome Club when we were hired. As it stood, it was just a loose conglomeration of freaks."

Our hands never separated.

"Ray, I'm so glad you walked into the Institute that Friday."

***

In 2006, after the pill piece years and the conceptual projects, I returned to the activity that first led me to the arts: painting. I was fully cognizant of the absurdity of resuming the antique practice of painting in the twenty-first century—applying sticky stuff to a piece of cloth with a device made of animal hair. I remember the snide remarks made by some fellow artists when I returned to painting. This comment was especially mean-spirited: "Did you go to the *art supply store* today, Ray? Painters in the aisles with their red plastic baskets picking up their little tubes of paint, brushes, charcoal sticks, rag paper, Belgian linen. It's pathetic. Everyone buys the same stuff and know what? Everyone's paintings end up looking exactly like, well… paintings! Nice, polite paintings. Surprise! Painting is for pussies." Want to know the sad thing? I thought this dig was just about right. Earlier, when my practice was conceptual, I pitied the poor painters. Their little rectangles were to me symbols of a diminished ambition and a truncated vision. And yes, art supply stores embarrassed me.

When I made my first pill pieces in 1997, I was deeply involved in theory and extremely critical of painting. Painting just couldn't live up to its exalted status. I was a devotee of every other discipline: product and package design, architecture, custom cars, cooking, fashion, whatever. It now seems absurd to me that the one culture I flatly rejected was my own, the one I labored in for so long and knew so much about. Theory turned me away from painting, but ironically, it also brought me home. Taking the anthropological view, I came to understand painting as just another practice, *not* the supreme human enterprise I once thought it to be. Yes, painting was just another subculture! Somehow, that little kernel of an idea became an incredibly liberating realization. It allowed me to return to painting and to fully embrace it, unapologetically, and with no holds barred. It was important for me to realize that painting isn't profound in and of itself (it isn't, as they say, *privileged*); like anything else, it can only be made magical and profound by the labor of magical/profound thinker-makers. Didn't Abraham Maslow say, "A first-rate soup is more creative than a second-rate painting"? This time, when painting beckoned, no resistance was possible.

My painting is a severe and private practice, reductive and abstract. It's an instrument designed to snag and extract phantom phenomena from deep brain recesses. Painting allows me to do two things that enchant me—to mess with form, the core of all things, and to explore the workings of my mind— both, in silence and without words, far removed from the pandemonium of the outside world and the posturing of the art world.

I like to imagine that I am no different than the early humans who scratched geometric zigzag patterns into mollusk shells 500,000 years ago. For now, for me, painting is indispensable, but I don't want to mystify or romanticize it, that's been done ad nauseam and much to painting's detriment. Most people do the cliché thing, compare painting to making love or the pain and pleasure of childbirth, but I never forget Victor's down-market take on the artist's struggle to create significant work. He said it was like crapping out a hard, dry turd.

All said, I must make clear that despite my disillusionment, my dissatisfaction, and my struggle with art and with painting these many years, it was and continues to be the focus of my entire life. Victor and I and a large band of like-minded art world travelers have no religion, no church affiliations, no club memberships, no hobbies, and little money. We gave everything to our struggle to create an art of intelligence, beauty, and integrity that is right for each of us at this particular moment. Art, like most things one pursues deeply, is an endless source of knowledge and self-discovery. In the end, it became our Holy Grail.

There's been too much talk about painting for too long. Too much theorizing. Yes, painting is a ridiculous activity, but, you know, if you love something, if you love painting, just fucking do it! There are no things unworthy of attention. There are no inappropriate subjects. Nothing is off limits. Nothing too low. Love trumps reason, theory, and the status quo. Love trumps all. It can raise a dead thing. That's where NoLab got it wrong, they didn't love anything.

Victor always kids me about painting and the severity of my work, and I kid him about sculpture and his mucking around with rocks and dead trees. "In all art schools *everywhere*," I would tell him, "haven't you noticed that painting departments are always on the top floor? The air is pure, the light crisp. Painting is sprightly and cerebral and, up there, painters are closer to God. Sculpture is always in the basement with foundries that belch gas and bleed molten lead. The air is dank. Hairy men carry heavy stones. Hell is just one floor down." I remind Victor that everyone's very first creation is a poop, surely something to be proud of; then, however, most of us mature and leave all that behind, but it is a well-documented fact that the unfortunate mothers who inadvertently create sculptors have all been overly enthusiastic in the potty training department. "Good boy, Victor. You did it! It's simply perfect. You're a genius."

Victor definitely has a chronic anal fixation. I think it's the sculpture thing combined with the Jew thing.

***

Woody had some news for us. Jeff Goldstone's credit card had been used in Richmond, Virginia to purchase gas and groceries. He also discovered that Kaylee's brother Evan lives in Richmond. Woody texted me Evan's phone number and address. This was the break we'd been waiting for. With high hopes, Victor and I caught the morning flight out of LaGuardia. Two hours later we picked up a rental car at the Richmond airport and drove downtown. Checked into the stately old Jefferson Hotel. We knew we picked the right place when we discovered *My Dinner with Andre* was filmed there. Agreed to celebrate later with amarettos.

We wasted no time. Victor phoned Evan as we drove to his apartment. No answer. When we got to the building entrance, Victor waited for someone to exit, grabbed the door before it closed, and in we went. Victor knocked on Evan's door. No response. He turned the knob. It wasn't locked. He pushed the door open and shouted, "Hello, Evan, hello!"

Evan was on the bathroom floor, his face bleeding. He looked like he took a good beating. We introduced ourselves, helped Evan to his feet and cleaned him up. Victor found a bottle of Absolut in a cabinet (booze he can always find) and over shots, we all calmed down and got to talking.

Evan told us that some biker types showed up, just an hour before we arrived, looking for Jeff, Kaylee, and Dave. He told the bikers he didn't know where the three were. As if pummeling him weren't enough, they took his computer, and cash too. He was pretty shaken up. The kid really didn't know where NoLab was, but he told us that Kaylee had visited him last week; she told him only that NoLab was working on a project and they were staying in the Fan district. We told Evan to call the police to report what happened and we headed toward the Fan.

The introduction of actual physical danger immediately altered every aspect of our little venture, our attitude, and our casual, if not completely irresponsible approach to finding NoLab.

9

We drove the streets of the Fan District, past grand old Victorian houses, up Boulevard, down Monument, past the equestrian statues honoring Robert E. Lee and Stonewall Jackson, and past a weird Arthur Ashe monument. We were searching for something, anything, a sliver of a shred of a clue, first feeling pretty incompetent, later feeling guilty for gorging on Cuban sandwiches and coconut risotto cakes from Kuba Kuba. Seems as if we drove past that little café at least a hundred and fifty times before we stopped. There was always a crowd, so of course, we just had to check it out. Really didn't want to be wasting our time and Pinky's money, but after two days of this, what the hell, we thought, maybe we should just settle into our ineptitude and start planning dinner. I must admit that we spent a lot of time on Yelp looking for interesting places to eat. "Hmm," I said, "what do you think—Edo's Squid or Buz and Ned's?" Victor slammed on the brakes, backed up and double-parked. Had he perhaps spotted two parakeets screwing in a cage in a dimly lit apartment?

"Ray, look here."

Victor pointed to a Chevy van with New York plates and a

bumper sticker that said *Eat More Possum.*

He said, "Halfway down the block we passed a parked car with New York plates and a bumper sticker that read *Keep the CHRIST in Christmas, the C-H in Chanukah, and the PAIN in Painting.* You know what I'm thinking?"

Victor's discovery made no sense…at first, then some tired old synapses began to fire.

"Yeah," I said, "Dave had an enormous bumper sticker collection."

"Uh huh," said Victor.

"So maybe they're here?"

"I think so. These aren't your run of the mill bumper stickers, Ray, they're the ironic artifacts of a hipster collector."

"So now we surveil."

"Yeah, our first stakeout."

"Excellent!"

***

We waited in the car listening to one of Victor's music compilations. Victor parked strategically, in a spot from which we could observe both the van and the car. We took turns on watch. The hours passed. Out of boredom, Victor and I took to counting the tattooed women. More here than we'd ever seen before. I shut off Victor's music and turned on NPR. You can only listen to *Beer, Bait, and Ammo* so many times, right?

Victor's phone rang—an awful cricket chirp. "Hi Cor. What's

up my man? Uh huh, hmm. That's not so bad. Are you kidding, I've had *thousands* of girls turn me down in my life…Hell no! That's the way it goes for everyone. Just invite someone else to the party—trust me—it will all work out…You're *not* a loser! You're awesome! I've told you many times, grit wins the day—remember? Hang in there! I'll see you this weekend, okay? Sure, if you like…dinner at Shake Shack. Yes! I'm getting hungry already. Bye Cor. Love you. No, I love *you* more!"

Victor has been entangled in relationships his entire life, married twice, numerous girlfriends, busted up Nam buddies, and for thirty years—Corey. It's been one theatrical spectacle after another. A Fellini festival. It's a miracle that Victor held down a teaching position and made a lot of good art too. I jettisoned all that crap to buy studio time. Life's a trade-off. Frankly, Victor's personal life looked like hell to me, but, as they say, "whatever floats your boat."

We were still waiting and watching as dusk settled. Victor left to get coffee and more risotto cakes. I stayed in the car on watch. The Fan, it seems, is a real neighborhood. People were walking dogs, jogging, relaxing on porches, going to friends' houses with six-packs and platters of food. Quaint. I saw someone approaching the van. It was difficult to see in the dim light, but damn, it looked like Jeff. Yes, it was Jeff! I got out of the car and walked toward him. He saw me approach and jumped into the van. I yelled. He didn't know it was me, just knew someone was heading toward him. As I approached the driver-side door he looked directly at me as the van jerked forward. Around ten feet away it came to a skidding stop. Jeff got out and walked toward me. We embraced, laughing.

***

Can't tell you how shocked I was that we'd actually found NoLab! I once saw a rusted, dented wreck of a car with the words "tuned by mistake" spray-painted crudely on its side; well that's exactly how I felt. Victor returned with the coffee and food and Jeff invited us into their rented house.

Jeff, Kaylee, and Dave were all there. I explained how we came to be looking for them, the call from Pinky, our trip to the Institute, Woody's information on Jeff's credit card charges in Richmond, and finally Victor's miraculous spotting of the bumper stickers. Kaylee, Dave, and Jeff didn't know that Kaylee's brother was roughed up. They were upset when we told them, but didn't seem surprised.

They told us they'd left Brooklyn because they were receiving intimidating emails and texts. They chose Richmond because they'd visited a few times over the years and, aside from Kaylee's brother Evan and a few former VCU art school grads, no one knew them—so, a good place to work undisturbed.

Kaylee said, "Remember the Hans Haacke piece that led to the cancelation of his Guggenheim show in 1971?"

"Of course, *Shapolsky et al. Manhattan* something or other," said Victor.

"Yes," Kaylee said. "*Shapolsky et al. Manhattan Real Estate*

Holdings, a Real-Time Social System, as of May 1, 1971. The exhibition was canceled six weeks before it was to open and the curator was fired. Haacke became celebrated for a show that never happened."

"And rightly so—he refused to submit to censorship," said Victor.

"As you guys know, the piece was a straightforward documentation of the transactions of the Shapolsky real estate network and its slum housing. At the time, some Guggenheim Board members were suspected of being connected to the real estate group, but nothing ever came of it," said Kaylee.

"Ownership was masked by a network of dummy corporations," said Dave.

"It took many years before Haacke's *Shapolsky* exhibition finally found a venue," I said.

"Yes, I saw it at the New Museum," said Victor.

"Okay gentleman, here's the story, Dia:Beacon got a huge gift to commission new work for a five-year programming series featuring activist art and design collectives, and we are one of the teams," said Kaylee.

"Congratulations!"

"Thanks, Ray! Well, we decided to see what would happen if we revisited the spirit of *Shapolsky*. Our piece will track the finances of today's ten wealthiest art world players." Kaylee continued, "Like Haacke's piece, this is a documentary project, but a lot has changed since Haacke obtained public documents to piece together the *Shapolsky* puzzle. The finances today are astronomical. The stakes are greater, and we have the internet, and social media…"

"And, we have Dave and his hacker friends," said Jeff.

"We've found more dirt than we ever imagined. You've got to see the email chains! These guys, and they are basically all guys, aren't your run of the mill collectors, some have collections worth hundreds of millions, even billions. They're the one percent of the one percent," said Kaylee.

"Our research has turned up lots of dodgy shit. Some of it will shock the public and stir up a media frenzy. It shocked us, and we already know all corporations are corrupt," said Jeff.

"Are you telling us you've hacked the emails of the ten wealthiest art world players and are going to publish what you've found?" I said.

"That's about right," said Jeff. "It's fucking amazing shit."

"No, that's nuts," I said.

"This isn't very smart," said Victor. "We just told you what happened to Evan—don't you realize that those goons were after *you*? And, depending how you obtained the email transcripts you will be subject to criminal liability, that's *if* hired persuaders don't get to you first."

"This is suicide," I said. "All it takes is *one* depraved CEO who cannot tolerate public scrutiny at this particular moment, one company that's into money laundering, one with unsafe employment practices in Bangladesh, one guilty of environmental crimes, just one, and you guys are screwed. And I'm sure most of these CEOs will simply not tolerate having their private emails go public. These people are connected. This isn't a game."

"Maybe so," said Jeff, looking at me, "but don't forget, in grad school, it was you who always told us to make work extreme enough to function as a parody of your own practice." Turning toward Victor, Jeff said, "And you urged us to 'go over the top,' to be who we are, but 'amplified,' to be '*molto* Goldstone,' '*molto* Kaylee'…so, we are totally committed. There's no backing out."

"I also told you 'no unwilling participants,'" said Victor.

"Jeff, are you doing this to hurt your father?" I said.

"Spare me the Freudian shit."

"Does he know about the piece?" I said.

"We didn't tell him, but he knows something," said Jeff. "Some people know; there's been a little leak."

"So, did he ask us to track you down because he was worried about you *or* because he wants to stop you from doing this piece?" said Victor.

"I don't know," said Jeff.

"Jesus!" said Victor.

"You two have gone soft in your old age," said Jeff.

"You know we believe in art that makes a difference and you know how much we care about you, all of you, but we can't support something this reckless. The incident with Evan is a warning. Think about it," I said. "Just think about what we're saying. I know you'll do the right thing. Now, what do you hear from your former NoLab member…what's his name? Lyonel?

Yes—Lyonel. How's he doing?"

"Good switcheroo!" said Jeff.

"Ray, always the diplomatic one," said Kaylee.

"Well," said Jeff, "We were just too white for Lyonel. He wanted to do politically correct social actions."

"That's a bit harsh," said Dave.

"No, that's just bullshit," said Kaylee. "Jeff's jealous, that's all."

"We haven't stayed in touch, but from what we hear, he's doing well," said Dave.

"He's doing more than well, he's rolling in samolians," said Kaylee.

"How so?" I said.

"Just a few years ago, about the time he left NoLab, he created a little app that started as a joke," said Dave. "He was a guest critic in Nina Spaulding's senior painting class. He suggested that the students didn't need all the time-killing crits, just an app. Point your smartphone at your painting, click and get an instant critique. Later, he realized that such a thing was actually do-able, and he went and built the damned thing. The app, *Instant MFA*, actually 'sees' the painting being critiqued, then it performs a pretty interesting formal analysis, discusses and displays related paintings from art history, and finally, it muddles through a critique of content—its weakest module— but all in all his little app accomplished its goal."

"And," said Kaylee, "it does it all with a good measure of style and humor. It offers universal truisms that would be useful to almost anybody in any situation. *Instant MFA* was an unexpected hit. Lyonel turned his apartment into a factory, producing critique apps for painting and an evolving roster of other disciplines. Needless to say, he's making a shitload of money."

"Yeah, I think I've heard about that app. Good for Lyonel! I always liked him," I said.

"Well, considering what *you guys* are planning now, I think Lyonel's departure from NoLab was a brilliant career move," said Victor.

"You know, Victor and I are gonna call Pinky, tell him we found you—and then tomorrow these two obsolete old men are flying home to New York. Come with us and speak to Pinky in person, clear the air, that's all we ask. Other than that, what you do is none of our business. Do your thing."

"Back to New York—no way," said Jeff.

"I think we should go. Maybe Pinky can help us," said Kaylee.

"I don't trust him," said Jeff.

"I'm with Kaylee," said Dave. "Besides, our first Dia allotment is gone already. Maybe he can float us till we get our second check."

"Ray's gonna tell him where we are anyway. Better to go see Pinky before he comes to us. Can't run forever ya know," said Kaylee.

"Okay, okay. I'm fucking tired of arguing, tired of hiding," said Jeff.

Kaylee, Dave, and Jeff agreed to fly back to New York with us.

Victor and I were prepared to drive to the airport in the morning. We agreed to pick them up at ten.

10

I was the designated driver. The plan: drive to the airport, drop off the rental car, a short flight home—easy. It's been almost a month since we began the search. I was feeling pretty good about what Victor and I accomplished. Pinky can't have any complaints—we found NoLab for him. I was already distancing myself from the whole search thing, looking forward to being in New York, my studio—my routine.

We got on I-64 and were making good time till three Harleys rode up beside us (well, actually, one was a Honda Goldwing). Typical-looking biker-gang types. Nazi-style helmets, bandanas, leather jackets, and vests with printed buttons and different kinds of patches sewn on. Victor had nothing but disdain for this kind of biker. He claimed their fat and sloppy bodies were unworthy of the machines they rode.

Two got in front of us, and the third guy, on our left, yelled, "Pull over, you have a flat tire."

Victor said to me, "Do NOT fucking pull over!"

I hit the brake and said, "They're slowing down. What the hell am I supposed to do? I'm not going to kill anyone."

"These are the guys that terrorized Evan. Just run them

down," said Victor.

"You *know* I can't do that."

"Suit yourself."

The three bikers forced our car off the road onto the dusty shoulder and then funneled us into the brush at the edge of the woods. The car bounced hard on the rutted ground. In the back seat, Dave and Jeff were screaming. "Jesus!" "Careful, careful!" "Oh fuck!" I stopped the car. Harley number one, with a spider web tattoo on his neck, approached. Victor got out; I hesitantly followed. In the back seat, Kaylee, Dave, and Jeff sunk down to the floorboards.

Looking at Victor, Harley said, "I don't like your face, old man."

"And I don't like your shit-eating Trump button," Victor replied. Harley made a fake move to hit Victor, but Victor didn't flinch. Harley moved closer to the left rear tire where I was standing and said to me, "And you, friend of Fuckhead, don't you know it's dangerous to drive with a flat?"

I took some time for a mock inspection and said, "It doesn't look flat to me."

He stared at me with dull unblinking eyes and said, "It's fuckin' flat." As he spoke these words he moved to the tire in question and unsheathed a large knife. It was pretty clear that he intended to make his lie a reality. Then it occurred to me, for the first time since the search began: this is the real fucking deal! This is really happening! Someone could get killed here! Knife to tire, Harley positioned himself to perform the deed—but nothing happened. Then—whoosh! Harley's head shot downward with an explosive force, pivoting from his waist in a perfect arc. An ugly grunt of a sound emanated from his nose cartilage and the bone of his eye sockets as they came in contact with the crown of the fender. It happened so suddenly, all I could make out was Victor's big hand on the back of Harley's neck, his thumb pressing into the blue lines of the web tattoo. The big guy hit the ground, his hands at his face. Victor calmly picked up the knife and removed a pistol from Harley's jacket pocket.

I supposed we were going to be torn apart by Sir Goldwing and Harley number two (his gut was comically massive, even by biker standards), all because Victor can never be reasonable. Victor always takes everything too far. But—perhaps—Victor did right this time. Maybe it was over the top or die.

Harley's pistol in hand, Victor checked the magazine. The two galoots who remained standing seemed as stunned as I was. Fat Harley (bald head, swastika tattoo on forearm) actually pumped up enough nerve to speak, "You're gonna pay for this, fuckers."

Victor said, "And you sir are going to throw all your weapons on the ground, *very* slowly, one at a time. You first, then your pal."

"Kiss my ass," said fat, swastika Harley.

"I would," said Victor, "but I really don't have all day."

Sir Goldwing made a sudden and stupid move. Victor shot him in the foot. With two bikers on the ground moaning, we gathered up all the weapons—two pistols, a set of brass knuckles, three knives, one straight razor, and a pair of nunchucks.

It didn't take long for Victor to extract the name of the person who hired them—just a little pressure strategically applied to a fresh wound with the still warm barrel of the gun. The first response to Victor's question, "Who are you working for?" was mostly a gasp. Eventually, the name Tereshchenko emerged, Lenny Tereshchenko. Victor punctured the tires of the bikes. We got back in the car and continued our drive to the airport. The scrubby bushes lining I-64 waved in the wind, cheering us on for miles.

For the first time ever, Kaylee, Dave, and Jeff had nothing to say. Now we all knew how serious NoLab's problem was and a lot more about my friend Victor.

***

As we drove on, I wondered who Lenny Tereshchenko was and why he sent bikers. And what's with the Goldwing? Didn't we warrant more nuanced antagonists? How about a sexy Mossad agent in an Armani suit, or at least a P.I. with a stutter and a butterfly collection? Wasn't it Armani who said, "Life is a movie and my clothes are the costumes"? Hey, Lenny, your bikers are in the wrong flick.

Memories of Victor's past rants interrupted my thoughts:

- Every generation of middle-class Americans seems to be getting wimpier. I know I'm not tough. I know I've had it easy. My father was tough. My father's father was dangerous.

- My friend Barry told me about his grandfather Isaac. He worked in a tailor shop in Brooklyn. On April 6, 1907, a man walked in and called him a dirty Jew. Isaac hit him with a baseball bat. The man died. Isaac left a note and disappeared. His family and friends never saw him again.

- Kids on tricycles wear helmets riding suburban sidewalks. Soon we'll all be wearing them every day. Universal all-day-helmet-use will be required by law.

- Removing the water-flow restrictor from a new showerhead is the most transgressive act left for middle-class Americans.

After one of these rants, I suggested that his 'good old days' of tough men also produced a lot of violent bullies and wife and child beaters. After a long pause, Victor responded melodically, "Never mind."

***

We stopped at a gas station and washed the blood off the fender. It was then a short hop to Avis. Returned the car (insurance covered the dents), and shuttled over to Departures. Richmond International Airport, hmm, where the hell was everybody? Was there some kind of bomb scare that we didn't know about? Guess not—there was an old guy in a sky blue jogging outfit at the US Air counter, a young couple at Caribou

Coffee, and a family of five, all dressed in camo, at the burger shop. I shouldn't be sarcastic, the lack of the usual airport crowds was positively luxurious. You could get used to desolate.

As we lined up for screening, placing our laptops, zip-locked liquids, and shoes in plastic bins, Victor whispered, "We sure owe the shoe bomber a debt of gratitude."

"Why's that?"

"For putting the explosives in his shoes…and not his underwear. If he put the bomb in his BVDs, right now we'd all be stripping down and walking through the puffer portal bare-ass with our undies held high, dangling from thumb and forefinger. Richard Reid was a very fine man!"

"I don't think we should be talking about this here, Victor, and besides, there *was* an underwear bomber."

"Really? Jeez! If you can think *anything* today, it's already been done or thunk before, eh? It's like if you make up a nonsense word and Google it, you'll find hundreds of books, restaurants, and companies with the exact crazy name. What's left for a bloke to do?"

There was a commotion behind us. Lots of yelling. Security guards started running toward the disturbance. I was ready to hit the floor. Anything out of the ordinary in an airport today is a potential disaster. Victor grabbed my arm, turned me around, and said, "Look, Ray, its Kaylee and Jeff and a TSA agent."

"Jesus," I said, "should we help?"

"Hell no! I'm going to New York. I don't want to be associated with whatever's going on at airport security. Not gonna jeopardize my trip home. They're big kids, they'll straighten it out. Besides, we weren't hired to be their bodyguards. The Pink man hired us to find them, that's all."

Just then I received a tri-tone text alert. "Okay Victor, here we go—this is from Dave: 'TSA says we are on the fucking no-fly list. Jeff demanded to see verification. Lost control. Might be detained.'"

***

As the Embraer 190 reached cruising altitude, Victor said, "NoLab must have ticked off someone quite powerful. I can't even imagine who could pull off a stunt like that—getting someone on the no-fly list. Isn't it managed by Homeland Security?"

"I don't know. Some federal security agency."

"Who the hell could arrange something like that?"

"Maybe it isn't related to NoLab's project," I said.

"That seems highly unlikely, don't you think? NoLab's involved in hacking some very rich people, connected people, some of whom might have secrets, and *coincidentally* they're put on the no-fly list?"

We ordered Bloody Marys, and I summoned the courage to bring up the biker incident. I asked Victor if we needed to worry about repercussions. He said, "No, no, no…maybe."

"Victor, in movies there may be no consequences for the hero's violent actions, but in real life there are police investigations, lawsuits, *and* there's revenge."

"Ray, it had to be done. Chill, my friend."

"Tryin'."

"It was completely obvious that the bastards meant to fuck us up. They began with intimidation. Sorry, but I'm not someone who's gonna passively walk into the fucking gas chamber. I just couldn't tolerate being humiliated by those slobs—so, that's why I did what I did. Or—maybe it was the big guy's Trump button. Whatever. Preemptive was the only way to go," said Victor.

"Hey, no need…I don't even want to think about what might have happened if they had their way. You may be a maniac, but you did good and I'm grateful. Touched, actually."

The plane jolted and suddenly dropped a few feet. One of the flight attendants hit her head on the overhead luggage compartment. They stopped serving for the remainder of the flight.

I take pride in my rationality. I see myself as a product of the great enlightenment project, but to be completely honest, there are times when superstitious thoughts bubble up unexpectedly. I am a nervous and fearful air traveler. Unfamiliar sounds make my thoughts turn to engine trouble. My rational self reassures me that bumps and sounds are normal, no need to panic. Sure, I'm cool with turbulence. I know how safe air travel is—statistically, nevertheless every bump suggests catastrophic engine failure, turbines choked by fat geese, or downdrafts so violent that the wings snap off and the plane begins to plummet. First I fear that something terrible happened and we are doomed (I think that's pretty normal), then I fear that simply *thinking* something horrific happened might actually cause the plane to crash (maybe not so normal). Yes, the images in my mind—playing in high def on a widescreen, with Dolby digital sound—might actually cause the plane to go down. I know how irrational this is, nevertheless I force myself to terminate all thoughts of oblivion in order to save the plane from destruction. This might not simply suggest that I am neurotic, which is, of course, true—it might suggest, counter-intuitively, some kind of weird, suppressed megalomania. Like, how can I possibly cause or prevent events with my thoughts? Who do I think I am, some kind of superhero?

Maybe my parents were right; I just have an overactive imagination. When I was a young boy, I would lie in bed waiting for sleep to overtake me. Staring into the darkness, scrutinizing my small desk, dresser, venetian blinds, lamp, and books, I imagined things lurking in the shadows, barely visible within the darkness. The dresser drawers had to be completely shut and the books all in place. When one of my crumpled socks, tossed haphazardly on the floor, just happened to take the form of a face, I couldn't sleep. I knew it was just a twisted sock-face, a mere resemblance, but its eerie presence held me in its vortex. I had no choice but to get out of bed to remove it and fold it till it was just a sock again.

***

Woody briefed us by email: Tereshchenko had an arrest record—mostly for bad checks and assault. He was a bouncer at the Rendezvous, a strip club in Long Island City. Woody also informed us that Tereshchenko had a Facebook page loaded with selfies. We took a look: Tereshchenko shirtless, Tereshchenko with buxom blondes, Tereshchenko downing Stoli at a glitzy nightclub, Tereshchenko with a Glock. Victor said, "What a douchebag."

***

The day following our return from Richmond, Victor came over to my loft to discuss the state of the search. No news yet from NoLab. I'd already called Pinky to tell him that Victor and I had concluded the search. His assistant said Pinky wasn't in. She would get back to me to arrange a meeting. Pinky didn't want our response over the phone or in an email message.

I had a margherita pizza delivered and opened an inexpensive Montepulciano. Victor said, "I'm so glad this is the end of our little quest."

"Yes, we're done. We did exactly what Pinky wanted. When his office calls to arrange a meeting, I'll try and get him together with Jeff for a sit-down—and that's that. That's it. Finito! And—Victor, you were great, really, I couldn't have had a better partner. I think it was a month well spent, and I thank you."

"Mutual, Ray, mutual."

We toasted, glasses clinking, "Mission accomplished!

Vittoria!"

"I only have one regret," said Victor.

"What's that?"

"I think NoLab's whole project was lame. Couldn't they be more original than a Haacke remake? Wish they made a humanzee. Now that would be fucking cosmic!"

My phone buzzed. It was Kaylee. She said they'd just arrived home. I switched to speaker. She didn't sound like her rock-solid self. "We ended up renting a car and driving back to Brooklyn because we were *all*, somehow, put on the fucking no-fly list and TSA wouldn't even tell us why. Jeff's lawyer told him that it might take a long time for us to get off the list, if ever. Jeff's freak-out at the airport didn't help our case. They held us for hours."

"Damn," I said.

When she told us about Peter Rademacher, her voice was quivering. Rademacher is a German collector, and one of NoLab's targeted art world luminaries. "He showed up at our place last night. He was with a giant muscle-bound dude he introduced as his driver, but the guy looked more like a bull terrier in a shiny suit."

Victor jumped into the conversation, "Rademacher. Jesus, I know that name. He's the infamous collector who graduated from stamps to Richter paintings."

"Infamous ballbreaker is more like it," said Kaylee. "He came right out and told us what he would do to us if we went public with his email correspondence. He could have had his *driver* do the dirty work, but it was like he enjoyed doing it himself. A real Nazi. It was gruesome. He ranted, got in our face, wouldn't let us say a word. I won't tell you what he said he'd do. You'd have nightmares. What was he infamous for, Victor?"

"Well, maybe a dozen years ago he purchased a rare stamp, *very* rare. There was only one known *Empty Ostafrika* in existence. Rademacher paid around two million dollars for it. There is a void where the image of a steamship belongs. Not many sheets were produced before the printing error was discovered. Some found their way into circulation but it was assumed that all had been lost over time. Around six years later, a second *Empty Ostafrika* showed up! A Boston antique dealer found it stuck to the side of a desk drawer. The Royal Philatelic Society authenticated it. Rademacher went berserk, literally stalked the owner of the other stamp, repeatedly attempted to buy it and repeatedly failed, had covert proxies try to buy it— failed. Then last year the owner died and it came up for auction at Sotheby's. The bidding was intense but Rademacher was going to have it at any cost. As it turned out, he didn't buy the little blue stamp for love. What he did next was chilling. He destroyed his new acquisition. He invited expert witnesses and had a video made documenting the burning of the stamp. It was as ruthless as an ISIS beheading. Once again, Rademacher possessed the one and only *Empty Ostafrika*. So listen, my friends, be warned, this is what you are dealing with."

"Freaky! What should we do?" said Kaylee.

"You *know* what we think. We made ourselves very clear—

drop this project and…If I were you, I'd announce it on social media," I said. In the background I could hear Jeff yelling, "Fuck you! We're gonna do it. You guys lost your balls a long time ago. Make your stupid little paintings! We're gonna do it, baby, gonna do something real!"

11

"What the hell are you doing in this dive, Victor? We have work to do, goddammit." The departing nurse gave me a disapproving look.

"Hey, I'm fine, fine, they're just running some tests about the jaundice. See, I took your advice."

"That's great. I'm glad. This is a good hospital."

"You know, Ray, most devout Christians and self-righteous born-againers aren't truly religious, least not in the way people were religious hundreds of years ago. Religion today is all show and no go."

"How's that Professor?"

"Because they come *here*. They come to hospitals and to doctors expecting science to cure them. They don't wait at home for God to stop their hemorrhaging and they sure as hell don't go to priests or ministers. They say they believe in God but their actions betray them."

"Maybe you're right, but, you damned well better know, Victor…I'm praying to God for good test results. When will they know?"

"I'm not sure. Tomorrow probably," said Victor.

"Do you have a good doctor?" I asked.

"He's good enough."

"What's that supposed to mean?"

"He's got a fucking MD degree. That's good enough for me. You know, every New Yorker will tell you, 'I have the best doctor. Voted number one by *New York Magazine*. Best gastroenterologist according to the L.E.S. Beekeepers Association.' Well, let me tell you something, there aren't that many best doctors in the world. It's a statistical impossibility. And you know what, I don't deserve the best doctor, nor do the countless slobs who tell you they have the best fucking doctor. The way I see it, we should just consider ourselves plenty lucky to have mediocre doctors."

"Well do you like your mediocre doctor?" I asked.

"Yeah, he's the best!"

"Tomorrow Florian."

"Ciao Raimundo."

∗∗∗

Migrating birds, drought-stricken gazelles, stalking leopards, pregnant horses. Animals know how to wait. Dogs wait alone all day in little apartments for the return of their masters. They wait for food and water, wait to piss and shit, wait to play, wait simply to be petted.

Waiting for a traffic light to turn green.

Waiting for the starter gun.
Waiting for the baby to arrive.
Waiting to hear if you were accepted to the college of
your choice.
Waiting to hear if any college accepted you.
Waiting to hear if you received a Guggenheim.
Waiting for the orgasm.
Waiting for the shit to hit the fan.
Waiting for the jury to decide your guilt or innocence.
Waiting while hungry.
Waiting in pain.
Waiting for the tears to stop.
Waiting fifteen minutes.
Waiting sixteen years.

There must be an infinite number of variations on the simple experience of waiting, but few can compare to the medical establishment's stark protocols. Waiting for the results of your biopsy, your HIV test, your daughter's MRI. Every bodily function goes awry. First you get the chills, then you have the runs.

Waiting Rooms. In the entire universe, could there be a more perverse architectural program? Class: Design a waiting room. "Waiting for what?" a clever student asks. "Just waiting," I reply.

What kinds of spaces might we expect? Isolation tanks? Pods filled with white noise? Chambers with banks of Valium I.V.s? Rows of Temple Grandin squeeze machines? How about geodesic domes where we can wait, levitated on puffs of perfumed air?

We didn't talk about it, but I knew Victor was waiting to

find out if his jaundice and stomach pain were symptoms of cancer.

***

The next day, around noon, I got a phone call from Victor. He was still in the hospital. I froze. Didn't want to hear the diagnosis.

"Hello, Ray."

"Hello, Victor." I waited.

"Today I looked more carefully at Tereshchenko's Facebook photos…"

"Okay. That's what you called to tell me? You're not calling about your health?"

"No, they don't have the test results yet. I'm calling about Tereshchenko."

"Jesus, Victor! You're still worried about that? I thought the search was over. Well, what?"

"Do you remember the picture of Tereshchenko drinking vodka in the nightclub?"

"The tacky looking place?"

"Yeah, the faux posh joint. Well, I took another look at the images, but this time I enlarged them. The club's called Czar's Palace. It's a Russian nightclub in Brighton Beach. In a few of the shots, I could actually see the faces of the people sitting at Tereshchenko's table—a very interesting group. You know who was there?"

"No. Trump?"

"No—Pinky!"

"No shit!"

"I told you the NoLab search smelled funny. Pinky threw too much money at us. He's not the concerned father he pretends to be."

"That's a bombshell…a fucking bombshell. You've got a good eye, my friend. You did good! Thanks, Victor. BUT–NOW–just get out of the damned hospital. I'll take care of everything else!"

***

On a rainy Thursday morning, armed with a little good news, I paid a second visit to Victor at Mount Sinai. After the fiasco of the NoLab search, and Victor in the hospital, I was looking forward to celebrating Victor's well-earned good fortune. He was getting an injection when I entered. The nurse attempted to close the privacy curtain, but, pointing to me, Victor said to the nurse, "No need, he can see everything. The more repugnant the better." Ignoring Victor, she closed the curtain. When the nurse left, someone from the hospital office arrived with a clipboard and a lot of papers. She had a list of questions. Victor told her I was family and okay if I stayed. She asked him all the usual things—address, insurance provider, relatives, emergency contact. She asked if he had an advance directive and his wishes concerning life support. She explained his patient rights. When she asked him his religion, Victor said, "Utilitarian."

"*Util*-itarian? No dear, you must mean Unitarian."

"No, I mean the U-*til*-i-ta-rian Church. You've never heard of it? Bucky Fuller is our minister."

"In the event of terminal illness, would you like Mr. Fuller to administer last rites?"

"Well, he's dead, so it wouldn't be very Utilitarian of me to bother him, so—no, no last rites, thank you."

The woman gave Victor her card and said, "Thank you, Mr. Florian. If you have any questions, please call." The door closed behind her.

Looking at Victor, I shook my head admonishingly and said, "That was amusing."

Victor said, "Whatever."

Heading toward the door, I said, "Let's start over, okay?" I went out into the hallway, returned smiling and said, "Good morning Victor! I suppose you've seen the new *Artforum*."

"Hi, Ray! No, I haven't."

"They must have sent a copy to your loft." Waving the magazine in the air, I said, "Prominently featured within this exalted journal is a fabulous article by Robert Storr about a funny old-timey artist by the name of Victor Florian."

"Hmm, really. I knew Robert was going to write something because he called with questions months ago—seems like an eternity now—but I didn't know when or where it would be published."

"Well sir, it's in *Artforum*—a five-page homage to the ground-breaking career of Victor Florian. It's amazing, true, and long overdue, so...congratulations Victor." I handed him the magazine opened to the article. Victor took the *Artforum* and sat on the edge of the bed reading.

"Well, I guess it's like the old saying, 'If you piss in one place long enough, you're bound to make an impression.'" Victor looked back down at the magazine in his hands and said, "Fuck them! The bastards always wait till you're dead or dying."

"What about the CT scan?" I asked.

"Not good. Pancreatic cancer."

"Fuck!"

We hugged in silence.

***

That night and the next few days I was too depressed to do anything or speak to anyone. Staying home with Jose Cuervo and waiting for Pinky to return my call was all I could muster. I scavenged a drawer of odds and ends and found a pack of way stale Marlboro Lights left ages ago by an unknown but blessed visitor. I boozed the day away, spent mostly on the couch; couldn't tell if I was half-awake or half-asleep. Reclining for hours, on my side, my head on a pillow, I examined the hairs on my arm. Up close, they are pretty monumental. I was in a grove of sequoias, but eventually, my scrutiny turned inward. I closed one eye and took in the vista; I opened it and closed the other eye—the image changed radically. Orientation A. Orientation B. Open. Close. Open, Close. I noticed that what I saw with my right eye was a bit cooler than the image I saw with my left eye. Yes, the image on the left was definitely warmer, redder. Is that normal or a symptom? I wondered.

Night two—again I drank too much; fell asleep on the couch and had a disturbing dream. I was seated in an airplane, people were boarding. I didn't know my destination; didn't even know what airport I was in. I was seated next to a woman holding a hissing badger. In the warped logic of the dream, I was more disturbed by the offensive amount of sweet perfume the woman wore. Thought I'd try to move to another seat after everyone boarded, but the boarding went on and on like circus clowns who endlessly, ludicrously exit a tiny car. A flight attendant walked by; I complained about the woman seated next to me. The attendant explained that the badger was an emotional support animal. As the passengers continued boarding, they talked loudly as if they were old friends on a chartered bus to Vegas. They spoke in German. I understand no German, but in this dream, somehow, I knew exactly what they were saying. As I watched the boarding procession, someone who looked like my father walked by. It was my father. The fact that he died more than thirty years ago didn't stop me from trying to get his attention. I waved my hands like a madman, but somehow, he failed to notice. He continued walking to the rear of the plane.

On day three I shaved and showered, dressed in jeans and my last clean shirt. Went out to get coffee. Walked for a while to clear my head. It was a sunny day and the neighborhood was humming. Vendors selling t-shirts, cheap hipster clothing for tourists, bongs and ornate glass water pipes. Stopped at the Starbucks on First Avenue for a tall coffee. Victor always seemed a tortured soul at Starbucks. He would only ask for *small*, *medium* or *large*, never *tall*, *grande* or *venti*. He said, "If they want me to speak Starbucks, they'll have to pay me." With coffee and scone in hand, I headed home to catch up on accumulated paperwork and email—just attempting to resume a daily routine.

Before I finished my coffee, Kaylee called. She was angry and agitated. "Not only did Dia:Beacon completely withdraw its offer to fund our big NoLab project, the fuckers dropped the entire five-year program, every art and design collective selected is now *out*, the entire project has been terminated!"

"Sorry, but you know, you have only yourself to blame,"

I said.

"Fuck you!" Kaylee replied.

"Well Okay, but a very wealthy donor probably got scared off by your project and threatened to withdraw some formidable Dia:Beacon funding or they had their lawyers scare the hell out of Dia—you choose. Or, maybe you scared…" She hung up. I didn't even get a chance to tell her about Victor.

***

Now in hospice, Victor was back home in his loft. Caregivers rotated shifts. When I arrived he was revising a pain chart with scotch tape and scissors. The standard hospital pain scale, one through ten, illustrated with ridiculous cartoon faces ranging from big smile, "no hurt," to big frown, "hurts worst," was being transformed by Victor with some images from art and cinema history printed from his computer. Now "no hurt' was the face of the angel in Bernini's *Ecstasy of Saint Teresa*, and "hurts worst," Gentileschi's *Judith Slaying Holofernes*. "This chart was just begging for a makeover," said Victor.

Victor was deteriorating rapidly, looking pretty frail. His skull was competing with his flesh for possession of his face. "Hey Victor, I brought you some Cherry Garcia," I announced. Victor smiled sweetly and said softly, "You know, Ray, the worst thing about losing a lot of weight is that it makes your nose look bigger."

"Okay," I replied.

"So, don't you wanna know the *best* thing about losing so much weight?"

"Sure, what's the best thing?"

"It makes your penis look larger!"

"You're funny."

"Ray, we've gotta talk. The doctors tell me I have only weeks or months to live…"

"Slow down, Victor, they have a lot of new protocols now…"

"No, Ray, not for what I've got, so let's just be realistic. I want to make sure you know how I want everything to proceed when I'm gone. You are my one and only beneficiary. You will get everything I have including the Pinky money, but most importantly I am asking that you be Corey's guardian. He's a good boy, Ray, and he's doing pretty well in his group home, but he needs love and guidance and someone to watch out for him and he always will. You are the only one I can trust with this. You are a lost soul but you have a heart aching to be loved. If you become Corey's guardian, I promise this, *you will be saved.* Tomorrow my lawyer will bring you documents to sign, and he'll explain the responsibilities of executor and guardian. Okay?"

Okay? Was there anything in the world I wanted to do less than become the guardian of a thirty-year-old man with

Down syndrome? Could there be an activity more alien to Ray Lawson than being responsible for another human being, and a seriously needy one at that? I'm the Ray Lawson who successfully avoided marriage, commitments, children, pets, even plants so I could have the time, money, and peace to make art. Once, in an exceptionally expansive mood, I thought I could handle the responsibilities of cactus ownership. The poor thing didn't ask for very much, but, somehow, I failed to provide its minimum requirements and it shriveled up and grew a nasty yellow fungus. Victor really misjudged me this time. Maybe he saw this as his last good opportunity to piss me off.

"Victor, you know how much I love you, but there's no way I can take on this kind of responsibility. Corey is a great kid, but I would be the worst caretaker, really, the worst. Maybe I can help you find some institution or…"

"No!" said Victor. "You have to do it. Please don't make me beg. It's not like I'm asking you to give me a final overdose of morphine. I got someone tougher than you to do that."After an awkwardly long pause, I nodded and said, "Okay, Victor, I'll watch out for Corey."

"No, Ray…I'm not asking you to watch out for him, I'm asking you to be his *legal* guardian. It's a very specific responsibility."

"I'd be the worst guardian. How about Savitha?"

"Savitha's just a kid."

"Hmm, what about Nina? She's so good with Corey.

She's got a strong maternal thing."

"You know I love Nina, but she's unstable. She can barely take care of herself."

"Can I think it over? Tell you tomorrow?" I said.

"Sure, tell me tomorrow—if I'm still alive."

Fuck Victor! Just a half-Jew, but he sure had the guilt thing going. I'm a loner, a pirate, a hobo, a monk. I'm not a freaking guardian.

A caregiver entered and with the push of a button she elevated Victor's bed, said it was time for his sponge bath. He bravely traded barbs with her. "Time for my martini, Perla?" She took off his shirt and said, "The only adult beverage for you today is Metamucil." Victor's chest was sunken, covered with age spots and tufts of white hair. His breastbone protruded alarmingly. Victor's great strength had wasted away. She gently washed Victor's face, his hands, his back, and his armpits. I stepped out of the room before she got to his crotch. So, this is what awaits us all. Perla opened the door, poked her head out, and said, "Done now. You can come in." I returned to the room. She packed up her equipment and said, "See you tomorrow, Victor."

"Tomorrow, Perla," Victor replied. When she left, Victor said to me, "She's a saintly one."

I looked into Victor's watery eyes and thought of all I had learned from him over the years, and all he had done for me. I'm sure as hell not into hero worship, but Victor was the only person I can ever remember looking up to. Damn if I didn't love this old man. As if in court, I took his hand and carefully articulated the words, "I will be Corey's guardian."

He squeezed my hand, placed it on the arm of the chair, patted it, then, slowly, he brought his hands together and bowed his head in the Buddhist manner.

Victor went on to explain his final wishes. He wanted no special life-support efforts, just a lot of morphine. When the time came, he wanted to end it all as quickly and efficiently as possible. He said, "Ray-o-vac, when you did the pill-pieces, why didn't you create a morphine-death-pill, hmm, it would have been your biggest hit—guaranteed to alter perception for all eternity." He continued to lay out his plans. Wanted to be cremated, the ashes dumped by the crematorium, not saved and not scattered. He did not want to be surrounded by friends and family as he lay dying. He didn't want a memorial service of any kind.

"Victor, services aren't for the deceased, they're for the living."

"Well fuck the living bastards," replied Victor. "And Ray, I don't want to have to put up with people feeling sorry for me or whining because I'm dying. I had more than my share of life—I have no complaints—it's been a blast. Whiners should shut the fuck up. Want to know another thing, Ray?"

"What, Victor?"

"Consciousness is the ultimate gift and I did my best to savor every experience. Just to be alive—what a feast—to have had the chance to see this big fucking crazy world for however brief a time. To see the sky, to feel the wind, to eat a ripe peach, to feel someone's body against yours, to make love, to read a book, to feel cold, heat—to cry, to run, to drive a car, get in a fight, get drunk, to love someone, to love things. People who believe in so-called miracles—like a cup rising up off a table, or water becoming wine—how pathetic is that? The real miracle is that there is a cup and you can see it and feel it, and even drink from it. Sentience is the big prize, the miracle of miracles that we all take for granted. You know what, Ray? I think mayflies are lucky to live their fleeting few hours—all emerging at the same moment, swarming upward, mating in air, then, perhaps, a quick death by a hungry cutthroat trout. What an amazing experience. Brief, yes, but so full—wired into the grand flow. In fact, a goddamned brine shrimp in a stagnant salt pond is blessed with sentience, even if all it can do is sense light and dark. Now I'll have that Cherry Garcia."

12

I finally got a callback from Pinky's assistant. Can I meet Mr. Goldstone in Central Park at three, Bethesda Fountain? I had to think for a minute, who the hell is Mr. Goldstone? Oh, Pinky. "Sure," I told her, "I'll be there."

Pinky showed up in a jogging suit. All Nike'd up. Looked more mobster than jogger. "Hello, Pinky. Why are we meeting here and why are you dressed like that? Never took you for a jock."

"I'm going incognito."

"Oh yeah, what are you hiding from?"

We found a bench and he began, "Let me try to explain. But first, Ray, thanks for meeting with me today. I heard about Victor. Can't tell you how sorry I am. What a disaster. I'm having some very special flowers sent."

"That's thoughtful, Pinky, but don't send flowers, really. I can tell you for certain, Victor wouldn't like that. He'd pitch them in the bin. Just a note would be nice. Email's best. You know he's not the traditional type."

"Okay, right, I get it." He paused, then said, "I know you want to tell me about the NoLab search, but let me just say:

Jeff called. I know where he is now. We already had a chat, and I'm gonna meet him, Kaylee, and Dave tonight. This wouldn't have come about if you and Victor weren't involved, so I want to thank you for what you guys did for me. I know it consumed a big chunk of your busy lives. I already deposited bonuses in your accounts, and, of course, I fully expect to receive a bill for any remaining expenses. Most of all, I thank you for being discreet."

A squadron of pigeons in matching gray gathered in front of the bench next to ours as an elderly man wearing a Homer Simpson t-shirt tossed breadcrumbs. I said to Pinky, "Well, thanks—you've been more than generous, and for that we are grateful, but we're also pissed. You weren't truthful about why you wanted us to find Jeff and NoLab. Frankly, we feel...used. You put us all in harm's way. If Victor were here and in his prime, I'm sure he wouldn't be so tactful, he'd probably kick your ass. So, what's the story? Why did you hire Lenny Tereshchenko to rough up NoLab? What's the deal, Pinky?"

Pinky bent forward, his head in his hands. After a long silence, he said, "I didn't hire Lenny to rough up NoLab. I would never do that! Would never do anything to hurt Jeff or any of you, never. Lenny was an accident. He's the boyfriend of Darya, my wife's personal trainer, and sometimes he'd drop her off and pick her up at the house. He was always polite and always offered to help out, seemed willing to do anything. I had him do some deliveries for me and then other little errands. I could tell he was tough, that was obvious. So, I asked him to see if he could find NoLab and get them to see me, and just scare them a little if necessary. I was being pressured by some heavy people to get NoLab to cancel its plan to go public with the hacked emails."

"Heavy? Like who?"

"Well, like the CEO of Anatolian Worldwide, for one."

"Oh shit! Peter Rademacher. He personally threatened NoLab."

"I know. I know. He came to me first, said if I didn't rein in NoLab, all hell would break loose."

"How did he find out that NoLab was hacking him?"

"Well, he's got kickass I.T. people. Anatolian *is* a tech company. As it was explained to me, their firewall easily detected NoLab's probe and they had no trouble tracking it back to its source."

"For Rademacher to be personally involved and threatening violence, he must have some serious shit to hide. Do others on NoLab's list know what's going on?"

"I think, by now they do. Rademacher told me he'd inform everyone NoLab hacked."

"Which means some other angry moguls might surface."

"Two others have already threatened me."

"Shit! If I were you I'd speak to NoLab about their current intentions, and then I'd hire security for you and your family. I know that sounds nuts, but NoLab must have inadvertently unearthed something hideous," I said.

"Early on, Rademacher attempted to talk to NoLab, but the three skipped town. Then he came to see me, and it wasn't pleasant. I hired Lenny but soon lost faith in his ability to find anyone or anything. That's when I asked you to help. Later, when you told me that you were going to Richmond to talk to Kaylee's brother Evan, I told Lenny and he arranged for some Richmond associates to find Evan too. Thought having both you *and* Lenny on the case would be like a little extra insurance. Unfortunately, Lenny's boys got to Evan before you did, and as you know, the stupid, inept, fuck-heads went rogue. I am so very sorry. I guess this is what they call *unexpected consequences*," said Pinky.

"Yeah, and your son Jeff, and Kaylee, Dave, Victor and I could also have been *unexpected consequences*. We could have been killed—and, just so you know, Lenny's so-called associates were actually biker thugs."

"I'm sorry. I really screwed up…and, by the way, I know something bad went down cause I had to pay hospital bills for Lenny's associates, one needed serious reconstructive facial surg…" Pinky's words were interrupted by an explosive shock wave, a violent burst of gray feathers and loud clucking. The entire flock of pigeons that so peacefully pecked on breadcrumbs at our feet, lifted upwards in a chaotic tempest of beaks and wings, expanding outward as it rose. I felt a hot wind on my face; dust burned my eyes.

Pinky began to run. What in hell? Then I saw the source of the disturbance above, it was a drone! A drone with a video camera attached. Someone's got Pinky under surveillance. As he sprinted for cover in a stand of trees, the drone whirred in pursuit. I walked slowly toward Fifth Avenue.

***

Victor's weight loss and physical deterioration accelerated dramatically. Pancreatic cancer is a fucking beast. Victor didn't want visitors, but they came anyway. His friends wouldn't accept being turned away. Victor almost always ended up enjoying the camaraderie. It was an endless progression of types, Vietnam vets, women of all ages, students, dock builder pals, and artists. Some arrived alone and some visited in groups. Carter Wilkinson, Crystal Breedlove, Lyonel Whitfield, Robert Storr and Woody Redman all made appearances. Liquor was always present, and some callers brought joints—for medicinal use only, of course.

One afternoon, Nina Spalding and Savitha Sharvani visited—one old friend, now a colleague, and one current flame. Nina was making martinis. Savitha was shaving Victor. He had shaving cream on the left half of his face. The right side was shaved smooth. Micah Gowen, one of Victor's Vietnam buddies, arrived. He abruptly rolled his wheelchair up to Victor's bed and Savitha jumped back.

Micah laid his head on Victor's chest and put his right arm around Victor. Victor made a face like *get this fucking madman off me*, but Micah hung on for a long, long time. When Micah rose up off Victor's chest, his eyes were red and wet, Victor's too. Then Micah bellowed, "Okay, that's over. Now there'll be no more sappy shit." He held up a bottle of Johnnie Walker and a large plastic sack. "Banh mi sandwiches, the pork belly kind. Today we celebrate life!"

Savitha finished Victor's shave and said, "There now, don't you look just grand!" Micah and Nina hooted their approval. As I poured Micah a glass of Johnnie Walker, Victor said to him, "Are you allowed to drive that chair under the influence?"

"Good one, Victor, good one. You know, I think you're lookin' quite fine. I don't think you got the cancer. I think you're fakin' it to get these foxy ladies feelin' sorry for you."

"Hey, Mr. Micah, it would take a lot more than cancer for us to feel sorry for Victor," said Nina.

Rotating his wheelchair around to face Nina, Savitha, and me, Micah said, "Let me tell you something about this old man…"

"No, no, no, Micah," said Victor.

"I wouldn't be here today if it wasn't for Victor Florian. I'd have died in Da Nang. I'd have just bled out like a pig in a slaughterhouse. VC mortar shells…"

"Jesus Christ," said Victor.

"This old man hauled me to a medevac helicopter."

"Okay, that's enough! Micah, I'm very glad you're alive, but let's move on," said Victor.

"So does that mean I can't tell them about the night with the Navy RNs in Hanoi?"

"Don't make me get out of this bed and kick your ass."

"Micah, let *me* pick up on the sexploits." Holding up a book, Nina continued, "In the sixties, the *East Village Other* was the raunchy alternative to the *Village Voice*."

"Oh God," said Victor.

"The *Other* had monthly 'slum goddess' centerfolds. From what I've heard, Victor shacked up with more than one of those goddesses of Avenue C. The writer Samantha Zee was, I believe, Miss February. She was just an aspiring poet when she hung out with Victor, but everyone knows that Victor is the inspiration for one of the characters, the sculptor Primo, in her recent novel, *Studio Life*. I offer you page thirty-five."

There were only a handful of galleries in SoHo in the late sixties, and the lofts and storefronts were primarily occupied by light manufacturing and warehouses. Primo's studio was previously home to ceiling-high stacks of cardboard boxes. It has been said that the reductive artworks of that era, involving the display, stacking, and scattering of raw industrial materials, were inspired by the merchandise in those cast iron district lofts. Days were teaming with activities and stock flowed out onto the sidewalks. Nights were dead still. Primo and his fellow artists painted their windows black so their occupancy couldn't be detected. They were illegal residents in commercially zoned buildings.

The East Village was only blocks away. The neighborhood, from the Bowery to alphabet city, was a lively, hippie enclave. Alternative lifestyles, counter-culture communities, free love, flower power, LSD, and pot. Timothy Leary, Baba Ram Dass, Scientology, Hare Krishnas, macrobiotic food, Vietnam, the draft, the anti-war movement, Black Panthers, Black Power, Janis Joplin, the Doors, Dylan, Hendrix, R. Crumb. It was a lot to handle in your formative years. It was exhilarating. It was dangerous. A lot of high-flying kids fell hard.

Primo possessed the soul of an artist. Astrid wanted to be a poet. They were tenement rats scampering through cooked cabbage halls, writing poetry, dropping acid, making art, making love. Ingrid and Primo screwed on hot, sticky summer nights till the cockroaches dropped from the ceiling. Along with the scent of burning cannabis, Grace Slick's voice floated from the airshaft: "One pill makes you larger…"

"Okay, that's enough for now," said Nina, closing the book.

Everyone applauded. Micah executed a loud catcall.

"You naughty boy," said Savitha. "And I thought I was your one and only."

The five o'clock hospice nurse arrived and said, "My God, what's been going on here? Well whatever, it's over now. Victor and I got business to attend to, *then* he really needs to rest. Okay, all?"

We cleaned the place up, nice and neat. I told Victor I'd see him soon. Savitha kissed Victor on the lips. Micah grabbed Victor's hand and said, "Hang in there papa-san." Nina shook his foot. Victor smiled.

***

Corey'd been through a lot since Victor was hospitalized— learning that his dad had cancer, recognizing how severe it was and how little time Victor had to live. How could the kid bear it? Victor wasn't just Corey's father—Victor was Corey's mother, brother, and best friend. He was a God to Corey. Luckily, Corey had a good counselor and they were meeting often during this period. I made contact with Corey's supervisor at work and with his counselor, generally preparing to transition to bill payer and guardian.

I knew Shake Shack was Corey's favorite restaurant, so I invited him out for lunch. Saturday was sunny; good weather for our outing. He said he wanted to get there on his own, said he knew how to take the subway to Twenty-third Street. When noon came but no Corey, I was okay. By twelve-thirty I was a wreck.

He arrived out of breath, his face all flushed, and as always, sporting an argyle sweater vest and wearing a backpack.

"Hi, Ray!"

"Hi, Cor." We did a high five followed by a low five.

"Let's get in line," said Corey, "I'm hungry."

"Me too."

In the queue, I asked Corey about his subway trip. He described his experience in great detail—the interesting people who got on and off at each stop—the singing panhandler, the blind woman, the guy spinning a basketball. We finally got our burgers and fries and found a table. Corey said, "I like the subway. I like doing things on my own. Today was good, no one hassled me."

"What does that mean, *no one hassled you?*"

"No one made fun of me. No one bullied me. No one laughed at me. No one stole my phone."

"Shit. How often do things like that happen?"

"Now you sound like my dad, with the bad words."

"Sorry, Corey. Well, how often?"

"Lots," Corey said.

"Lots! Now I'm getting angry! How do you deal with that?"

"I ignore it like Dad taught me. He said those people are a-holes, but *he* never ignored those people. Once he even hit someone who called me a retard. The police came and Dad got in trouble."

"Why doesn't that surprise me? Well, at least you know it's because your dad loves you so much."

"Dad's going to die."

"Everyone has to die sometime, Cor. Your dad will have had a good long life. He did more cool stuff than ten average people put together. My dad died when I was not much older than you. I thought it was the end of the world, but you know what I learned?"

"What?"

"I learned that he never completely died. He lives on, in my mind and my heart. I think of him every day and remember all the good things, all he taught me, and how he loved me—and, Corey, it will be the same for you. Your dad will always be with you. And, you know, he taught you to be tough. You and I will get through this together." Corey toppled toward me, wrapped his arms around me. I held him tight. I said, "Core, you'll be okay. I'm here for you now."

After lunch we headed up to Central Park, did some people-watching and tossed a Frisbee for a while—then I put him in a cab for home. I said, "You have my number— call me any time. I love you, Corey."

13

I visited Victor in hospice quite often during those twilight days, sometimes with Corey, sometimes with Allana, sometimes alone. Talking was becoming difficult for Victor. He would ask me to read to him, requested old Huck Finn—Corey liked it as well, and when he was present I read to them both.

On the visit that was to be our last, I interrupted Victor fiddling with his iPhone. "Hi Victor, am I disturbing you?"

"Ah, no. Just looking at my Instagram." Victor was the least likely person to be engaged in social media, but some grad students had set up an account for his artwork and encouraged him to use it. Victor frequently railed against the new online gallery and auction sites and their feature stories: "Trending Now," "The Ten Best Booths at Art Basel, Miami," "Art that Captures the *Hygge* Vibe Everyone is After," "Great Investments: Artists on the Rise." OMG—the worst aspects of the art world, now available to everyone, thanks to social media. Nevertheless, Victor had over five thousand devoted Instagram followers.

Victor said, "Instagram is pretty fascinating, it reminds

you how much good, serious art there is, but also that there are mountains of God-awful crap. The young artists on Instagram seem amazingly, obliviously happy. They're posting selfies, cute cat pictures, shots of beautiful vacation places, fabulous food from hip restaurants. When I was a kid, my family was poor. We lived in a factory town in northern Pennsylvania. We were lucky to have enough to eat, but my mother never let us eat in public, never wanted to show off in front of neighbors who had less, never wanted to make them feel inadequate, and we always took in friends and family in need. Don't these kids know others are suffering while they post their perfect lattes? And— even worse—they are making art look like fun. All these artsy kids in Bushwick are like happy preppy campers, doing studio visits and residencies, promoting each other's little shows. Jesus Christ, art shouldn't be fun—it should make your liver bleed. Where's the humility? The angst?" Victor sipped some water through one of those bendable hospital straws; he sat still for a while, then pointed to me and said, "Forget all that." He waved his hand sideways and said, "Erase!—I'm glad the kids are having fun, let them enjoy! Really!" Then, after a long pause, he leaned toward me and whispered sheepishly, "But...I wish their fun didn't have to be so fucking fluffy."

"You mean wholesome?"

"Yeah, wholesome and frivolous."

I told Victor all about Kaylee's angry phone call, the

cancellation of NoLab's Dia:Beacon exhibition, and NoLab's inability to to get off the no-fly list; about my meeting with Pinky and his piss-poor apology, Peter Rademacher's threats, Pinky's relationship to Tereshchenko, and the pretty funny image of Pinky running for shelter with a drone buzzing in pursuit. Victor took it all in, but was clearly uninterested, just nodded a lot and said, "Stay out of it, Ray. Keep your distance. If NoLab releases those emails, it'll be a shit storm."

Victor had more important things on his mind. He was on the edge of the abyss and he wanted to talk. In a hoarse whisper interrupted by a dry cough, jumping from topic to topic, from high to low, willy-nilly, he philosophized. Was it a morphine-induced rant or just Victor being Victor?

"You know, Ray, this Donald Trump thing is really getting me down. Lots of folks are being duped by this pathetic buffoon. When Americans think *winning*, whatever that means, is what life is about, we're fucked. The people who support Trump are as deluded as suicide bombers. Our worst enemies couldn't do a better job of spreading fear and undermining faith in our government than Trump and the entire Republican crew.

"I'm not a fan of papers like the Daily News, but I must say, their front pages during this campaign are warming my tired old heart. Full-page images and giant text. Trump and Sarah Palin pointing at each other with the headline blasting, 'I'm with Stupid!' Image and text combined make the most potent form of communication ever devised. I really think the editors responsible for this are fucking brilliant—they should get MacArthurs and those front pages should be in the next Whitney Biennial—I kid you not. Barbara Kruger, shove over!"

Victor paused for a long while, then got a second wind.

"You know, Rayathon, it's the things that can't possibly work *but do* that amaze me. Like, there is no way a Boeing 747 with more than 500 passengers, plus luggage, and cargo—we are talking over 400,000 pounds—could ever get off the surface of the earth. Just no way. A little less air pressure on top of a moving wing—Mr. Bernoulli, spare me.

"And what about Manhattan? Getting the food *in* and the shit *out* every day for over eight million people. Getting everyone to their jobs and then home daily. Entertaining them. Stacking them all, one above the other, in their little apartments. Can't work. It's only a matter of time before the plague will wipe out the entire lot.

"Then, of course, there's the human body, reproduction, the whole ball of wax. Nothing as complex as the human body and as surreal as sexual reproduction could ever work. If you think an organism can exist that can think and talk and reproduce itself, and, by the way, it happens to have over thirty-seven trillion cells working cooperatively, well you are quite a dreamer. Hey, and while we're at it, as far as I'm concerned, all biological life is impossible. And, concerning the big one—the Universe—wouldn't it have just been more logical and easier for all concerned if nothing *ever* existed?

"Well, all these things that can't possibly work are just running along like big dumb, happy dogs.

"Maybe our problem is just that the human race hasn't fully evolved. We tend to think we are completely resolved creatures, you know—the last, definitive, perfect version— but, hey, it may take another five hundred thousand years to get us right, if ever. There is, though, one person who has evolved to a higher level, Ray, know who that is?"

"Uh, hmm, no. Uh, the Dalai Lama?"

"No, but good try. It's Barack Obama. If I hear someone bad mouthing that man, I sure as hell don't keep quiet. I'll have none of that racist claptrap. The only reason I haven't blown my brains out is Barack Obama's presidency...and, well, also gelato...and of course, the glorious women in my life, my Nam buds, and let's throw in Pope Francis, the Magliozzi brothers, Blossom Dearie, and, let me see here... linguini with clams, panna cotta (without any topping, doing that to panna cotta is just plain nasty), and booze, any kind—fermentation is, of course, the most wondrous of all human discoveries."

"You're scaring me, Victor. You're starting to sound like the old Carl Reiner/Mel Brooks routine, the interview with a two thousand-year-old man, remember? Reiner asked Brooks what the greatest discovery was in two thousand years of human history and Brooks answered, 'Saran Wrap.'"

"Yeah, I remember that. So funny. When Corey was around ten years old I encouraged him to do stand-up. He was a natural ham and I thought the world could use a Down syndrome comic. Well, Cor wasn't cut out for stand-up. It's a very rigorous practice, ya know—but, when he was about six he did have great success cracking up every adult he met with the single kid's joke he learned, 'What's invisible and smells like a carrot?' Answer: 'A bunny fart.' Corey could really tell it. You know, the Cor loved *show & tell*. He just naturally tapped into seminal truths. He got it so right: *show & tell* is pretty much the essence of art—and life in general. You must be excited about something in the world, bring it into school or a gallery or wherever, and share your excitement with others. I think if I could do it all over again, I'd make art school one hundred percent *show & tell*. You know, if you're not passionate about things, you're a goner."

Victor looked down at his phone, still in his hand, and said, "You know what I like about my iPhone?"

"I'm not really supposed to answer that, am I?"

"You are wise, dear Raymond. Well, I heard this discussion on NPR the other day, some experts were discussing the social impact of smartphones, you know, like all the things smartphones have replaced—but, no one said what I was thinking. *I* love my iPhone because it allows me to believe I live in the future, and in that future I'm surrounded by compassionate, rational, intelligent people— yeah, people so intelligent and inventive that they are capable of creating this little piece of magic." Victor lifted his phone and gave it a quick shake. "This thing makes me feel good about myself and the world…well at least for a moment, because then I look up from the phone and see the ugly truth: the world I live in is more like the past…and it's barbaric."

After an extended bout of coughing, Victor continued, "Hey, Ray, you know I once heard Dick Hebdige say that the porters' uniforms at the Athens airport were emblazoned with the word METAPHOR. Do you think that could be true? Maybe I imagined it."

"You mean in Greece?"

"Yeah."

"Sounds good to me."

"Okay, wanna know what else has kept me from splattering my brains? You, Ray Lawson, and my precious Corey, but that need not be stated, right? So, let's throw in Duchamp, Willie Nelson, Bucky Fuller, Mark Twain, Warhol, Corbu, Luis Barragan, soft shell crabs…Ruth Bader Ginsburg, Maine lobsters, a good Barolo, oh, never mind, I already said booze. Ospreys, dolphins, Eva Hesse, Dolly Parton, George Jones…and let's see, oh yeah, Beckett, Nabakov, Melville, Freud, the Buddha…"

"You've never been anywhere near suicide," I said.

"Oh…I guess you are *exaggerating*. You're dying of cancer—you could at least try to be mildly depressed."

"I heard that David Smith, when he was too depressed to talk, would draw pictures of bacon and eggs, a coffee cup, or whatever on a napkin and push that napkin across the counter to order lunch at the diner near Terminal Ironworks. That reminds me, dear Ray, would you do me a big favor?"

"Of course. You name it."

"Next visit, bring me a plate of bucatini from L'Artusi, okay? Bucatini with pancetta and chilies. I've got a wicked craving."

"That's easy, the bucatini will soon be yours—and I'll bring a nice red to go with it."

"How about a chianti classico."

"You're a cheap date, my friend."

"Okay, what did I want to get back to? Yes, President Obama. He's surely the smartest President ever. He's just the best. He's ethical, has a reasoned and deliberate response to things, and a supremely dignified demeanor. I could never in a million years want a better person to represent me and this country.

"And Ray, how did Bush and Cheney ever sleep at night? If you're happily cruising down the highway and you run over a squirrel that dashes out unexpectedly, you feel like shit, right? Have you seen the devastating injuries these soldiers come home with? How the hell could anyone possibly live, knowing they were responsible for that?"

I said, "Remember when Obama was campaigning, Kaylee had a bumper sticker made for you that said, *Gun Totin' Rednecks for Obama.*" Victor smiled.

"Yes, Ray-zee, and remember when I taught a term as a visiting tutor in Birmingham. It wasn't my first trip to the U.K., but it was my first time living and working there. I think it was in '97. I took the train from London to Birmingham and back weekly, and I lived in a flat in Duncan Poole's south London estate. Estate, *sure*, it's called a tenement here, right? Well, I'm embarrassed to tell you that I brought a shit-load of stereotypical notions with me on that U.K. trip. The Queen, Buckingham Palace, Tower Bridge, WWII movies, the Beatles, Carnaby Street, Saville Row, proper British accents, and impeccable manners. Needless to say, I returned home with a greatly expanded view of the small plot of England that I got to know a bit better. Yes, it kinda resembled the touristy things, but it was also grittier, more violent, and more inebriated than I could ever have imagined—rougher, by far than the New York I knew—but also more vibrant than the fantasy England I constructed, and more disturbing.

"These many years later I remain ashamed of how misinformed I was. Couldn't I have just seen a Mike Leigh movie for God's sake? Now, I am far more ashamed of my misunderstanding of the citizens of my very own country. As a first generation Italian and a second generation

Hungarian Jew, I must admit to some deeply embedded notions about white Protestant America, what I imagined 'real' Americans to be. They were decent, law-abiding, moral, and perhaps a bit boring—I guess I watched too many episodes of 'Leave it to Beaver.' Sure, I was, and remain well aware of the existence of racism, sexism, homophobia, and xenophobia in America, but by and large, somehow my attitude toward my fellow Americans remained a positive one.

"Now, Donald Trump is encouraging Americans to flaunt their ignorance—to join the mob, to conjure up scapegoats, to hate. How can so many of these 'Leave it to Beaver' Americans support a man like that, a thug, really? Have they always been fucking racist hate mongers? Could I…could so many of us have been *that* blind?

"We are living a nightmare in which a man all too close to the Presidency of the United States holds views you wouldn't tolerate in your barber or your plumber. Trump's a man who's lived a life of pure greed."

After a fit of coughing and a sip of water, Victor continued, "Ray, who was that famous Scandinavian dude who explored the Arctic? He equated civilization to a kind of rock tumbler. You know, you put all these rocks of different sizes and shapes into the tumbler and they are ground down to sameness. They all come out looking alike. Well, this explorer believed that civilization did that to people, too. We are all tumbled, battered, and eroded by our interactions with each other. Worn down to a kind of generic uniformity. Only living alone in nature could permit our unique selves to flourish. Well, I've been in the tumbler long enough. It's time to go, before the craggy topography that makes me Victor Florian is completely gone, before I'm a tiny sphere, devoid of all Floriana."

Victor's words, barely audible, came slowly now. "You know I've always liked strong flavors and a good fight, and I put up with all kinds of craziness, but my dear Ray-sun-det, the world has gotten too ugly, even for this ornery old man. Trump's ascent gives one a hint of how the Jews in Germany must have felt watching Hitler's rise to power. The Trump candidacy will foul the air and stain our flag for years to come.

"Today I'm ashamed to be an American and disgusted with what our country has become. If I weren't dying I'd go to Colorado and stay stoned for the rest of my life."

Victor's voice was drifting off. After a long pause, he said, "Ray, this is the perfect time to yield the floor. I couldn't have planned it better if I tried."

Now exhausted, Victor closed his eyes and fell asleep. I kissed his forehead and left.

***

Other than a brief mention in *Art in America*, not much happened when Victor died, and that's exactly what he would have liked. His body shut down the morning of November 5th, just three days before Donald Trump upset Hillary Clinton to become the forty-fifth President of the United States. Yes, Victor timed his departure well; he would never have to see his despised Trump in the White House and his beloved America disgraced.

I remember Victor's excitement when the Washington Post released the *Access Hollywood* video of the lewd conversation between Trump and Billy Bush—Pussygate. Victor said, "Awesome! Now everyone can see what a true pig this guy is. And only two days before the next debate. Trump's goin' down!" Well, we all thought that would be Trump's demise, after all, people weren't idiots. How wrong we were!

***

Some students created a memorial Facebook page for Victor. They invited other students, colleagues, and friends to reminisce and recollect. Lots of sweet messages: "We'll miss you, Victor." "Thanks for your love and wisdom." "Hey man, you can't go, I owe you a beer." All more or less what you might expect, but the pithy, wise-weird things Victor said in classrooms and bars over the years, as posted on the memorial page, were more revealing. These are my favorites:

"You know squat" was on the page because it somehow

means the same thing as its opposite—"you don't know squat." Victor loved ambiguous expressions. He was a maven of what he called linguistic *mishegoss*. He collected crash blossoms, those hilarious newspaper headlines with alternate readings. One of the greats that made the page: "Red Tape Holds Up New Bridge." He often told his students, "If you don't love ambiguity, baby, you're in the wrong game."

He delighted in the legendary story about the Oxford philosopher J. L. Austin who asserted at a lecture on linguistic philosophy that there are many languages in which a double negative expresses a positive, but none in which a double positive makes a negative. The esteemed philosopher Sidney Morgenbesser, sitting in the audience, muttered sarcastically, "Yeah, yeah."

Victor had more enthusiasm for more things in life than anyone I ever met. Van Gogh said, "To know God is to love many things." If that's true, Victor was the Pope.

He was a fan of the corniest jokes; his complete repertoire was probably established by fifth grade. One student listed this as Victor's most frequently told:

Question: "Why is shit tapered?"

Answer: "So your asshole doesn't slap shut."

It's a real sculptor's joke (right up there with Rodin's aphorism, "Sculpture is the art of the lump and the hole."). It celebrates earthy materiality, Euclid, and Newton all at once.

Victor insisted that a story about a Seeing Eye dog revealed the naked soul of New York and he told it often: "I was in a cab in midtown when a blind man with a Seeing Eye dog was crossing the street, directly in front of the cab. The light for the cab turned green and the blind man was still in the middle of the intersection. The cabdriver started honking his horn. I said to him, 'What are you doing, can't you see the man is blind?' The cabby responded, 'The dog should know bettah!'" I heard Victor tell this story many times, too many really. He said he heard Johnny Carson tell it on the old *Tonight Show*. Once, after telling it, Victor looked at me and, in all seriousness, said, "Ray, how do blind people pick up after their Seeing Eye dogs?"

Victor's nutsy business ideas were also included. For a couple of years, he went around telling everyone he was going to open a kishka restaurant called *Just Kishka* or alternately, *Kafka's Kishka*. One day it was a drive-through take-out joint he would operate out of an old barn he saw for rent in Sag Harbor, other times it was going to be a full-blown restaurant in the City, later it was a franchise that he *just knew* would go global. *Just Kishka* would serve kishka of course, and nothing but kishka, the classic, but at times Victor said he might bow to the zeitgeist and offer some trendy variations like Moroccan tagine kishka, and moo shu kishka. For the kids, kishka sliders and shakes. Victor was a pretty funny guy, but he explained his plan to a lot of people in great detail and with total solemnity. Whenever he met some wealthy collectors at a party or an opening he tried to get them to invest. Since most of his victims had no idea what kishka was, this was all perversely amusing, *and* if you *did* know what kishka was (an Eastern European delicacy consisting of fat and paprika stuffed in a cow intestine), you knew how really weird Victor was.

He often told students how John James Audubon caught hummingbirds to use as models for his illustrations. Audubon put wine in the nectar of flowers and then, with his bare hands, just scooped the inebriated little angels off the ground.

Considering the serious, erudite, and profound things Victor has said over the years, it's funny what the students remembered. As I reread the Facebook page, it occurred to me that this crazy stuff might actually be a deep indicator of Victor's spirit. He was a vulgar little Zen master. You just won't find the likes of Victor Florian around anymore. Can't be taught in a grad seminar or a professional practices class.

14

Corey was devastated by the news of his dad's death. When I got him to settle down he hugged me and wouldn't let go. He smelled like wet wool and sour milk.

Later that week I drove to Corey's group home to take him to the funeral parlor to arrange for Victor's cremation. I told him he didn't need to go, shouldn't go, but he wanted to be there. When he's determined to do something, there's no dissuading him, just like his old man. As we walked to the front entrance, Corey grabbed my hand and held on tight. Damn, his square, stubby fingers were strong.

I remembered Victor's hand on the biker's neck and I understood that it was Victor, now, leading me, pushing me, into the wet, messy, heart of life—the sacred, pulsating core of things that I have for so long conspired to avoid.

A yellow cab pulled up. Out stepped Allana. With her pure white hair and powder blue dress, what a totally delightful vision. She ran over, hugged Corey, kissed me, and grabbed my free hand. Like the tendrils of a young vine, her delicate fingers encircled mine.

Together we marched up the granite steps, past the white

columns to the foreboding gray doors of the Bennett and Chandler Funeral Home. A strange sensation inched up my arm, a subtle vibration. It was the oscillation of the helices—from hand to hand, from Corey, through me, through my chest, my heart, my very soul to Allana and winding back again. I looked at Allana—she felt it too.

The gray doors were no longer a terminus. They beckoned. The three of us climbed upward toward a new beginning.

***

Allana and I are living together. Victor wouldn't have believed it. Hey, *I* don't believe it. Can't even remember having ever been this content. With her dog, Becher, we moved into a spotless new apartment in DUMBO— triple pane windows, granite countertops, A.C., stainless steel appliances, balcony, the whole deal—as close to my fantasy Swiss venereal disease clinic as you can get around here. It was surprisingly gratifying to go for middle-class ease and comfort, after all those years shunning bourgeois trappings. Our big snub of domesticity was, you know, our certification of seriousness, our badge of dedication, our rebel yell. Now, Allana and I shop together. For God's sake, you'd think we were young newlyweds.

On the balcony, looking across the East River this glorious night, I could see Manhattan all lit up. I lit the grill and threw on some corn, onions, eggplant and peppers. It had been a long day, Allana had prepared for her exhibition at the Luce and I'd spent the morning with my Columbia grads. Allana poured two glasses of wine and we toasted Victor. Allana and I enjoyed just being together, that was more than enough.

"Ray, I've been thinking."

"Uh huh?"

"We have an extra room. So, what do you think about having Corey come stay with us?"

"Why not? I'm sure he'd like to visit. Bet he'd dig the pool and gym."

"I'm not thinking about a visit, I'm thinking about him living with us."

"Permanently?"

"With Victor gone, he's gotta be lonely, and living in a group home can't be easy."

"He might feel more comfortable in that group home than you think."

"Well if you don't want to have him stay here, that's that, but it's safer here. I don't like where he is in Queens."

"I'm his guardian, and I really care about Corey, but even Victor didn't live with him. Victor felt Corey was better off learning to be independent, needed to learn that—but, let's invite him to stay for the weekend and see how it goes, Okay?"

"Good idea, Ray. Let's see how he responds."

***

"This place is way cool," said Corey. He seemed to be enjoying the new apartment and family life, and why not? Allana and I were as well. He spent Saturday morning playing with the dog and binge-watching *Blue Bloods* on Netflix. That evening we walked over to Gran Electrica for tacos, I indulged in a mezcal, and we still had time to get to Jacques Torres for hot chocolate and ice cream sandwiches. Where have these easy pleasures been all my life? It felt good. Damned good.

The three of us walked home in a cool breeze. By the time we got upstairs, we were all exhausted. Corey went to his room. Allana turned on the TV news. I enjoyed my evening vodka and picked up the novel I was rereading, *Alone in Berlin*. Since Trump won the election, I was trying to avoid the news. It was just too painful watching people responding to a madman as if he were normal. Such a charade will surely drive us all insane. Allana punched my arm hard and said "Look! Look!" I turned my attention to the TV and saw a familiar face flash by. It was Pinky! The report just ended.

"What's going on?"

Allana whispered, "Your friend Pinky…they said…oh my God. He's dead!"

"What? What happened?"

"Auto accident, just caught the last few words," said Allana.

"Are you sure?"

"Yes, I'm sure. They said Stuart Goldstone died early this morning in an auto accident."

"Jesus!"

That night, despite booze, relaxation techniques, and breathing exercises, I just couldn't fall asleep. Checked Google—nothing more there. The shocking news of Pinky's death along with the image of Pinky fleeing the drone in Central Park were on replay and I couldn't shut them off.

***

Allana regularly eats yogurt or oatmeal for breakfast, but puts up with my unhealthy Sunday ritual of bacon and eggs—cowboy eggs, that is. Cook the eggs in the fat from the bacon, and just rough them up a little in the pan, that's all. These are not your picture-perfect fried eggs, nor your fluffily scrambled yellow clouds. These are ugly, blackened things, but you only have one pan to wash. Add *The New York Times* and you pretty much have it all. Victor used to tell his students how to make baklava: cut the full Sunday Times into two-inch squares, so you have a bunch of little stacks, soak them with honey, sprinkle with chopped walnuts—voila—sweet baklava—knock yourself out!

The only way I can describe Corey's entrance into the kitchen is to say *he moseyed on in*. His hair flamboyantly disheveled, pajamas on inside out, still half asleep. An endearing look—really. Becher raced around the kitchen, bumping off the walls and counters.

"Good morning," Corey said.

"Sleep well?" said Allana.

"Yes, thank you."

"Good morning, Corey. I made some delicious eggs for you, bacon too. Hope you're hungry."

Corey looked at the pan and said, "Yuck!"

"Yes, yuck," echoed Allana, pouring hot water into the Chemex.

"Do you have Froot Loops?"

"Hmm no, but we do have bran flakes. They'll be good with sugar on them," said Allana.

"Double yuck," said Corey.

"Oatmeal? Yogurt?"

"No thanks."

"I'll get some Froot Loops at the corner store. How about that?" said Allana.

"I'll try the weird eggs."

"Now you're talking!" I said. "You're a true Florian." Our little family enjoyed its first breakfast together. A *Car Talk* rerun was on NPR. Accompanied by lots of laughter and some snorting, the Magliozzi brothers were addressing the problem of a call-in guest who wanted to know how to avoid daily electric shocks when sliding off the front seat while exiting his car. As I recall, their first response was to accuse the caller of wearing cheap polyester suits. Finally, they told him to attach a wire with alligator clips from the dashboard to his jacket lapel. Then, *after* getting out of the car, undo the alligator clip, and that's it, no shock!

Victor always said that these two crazy brothers did more to relieve our collective psychological stress than all the shrinks and meditation in the world.

Corey said, "These eggs are good," and asked for more. "Bacon too, please."

"I told you they were good. They just look funny. And *that's* a lesson, ain't it?"

"Don't say ain't!"

"*That's* a lesson too."

"Ha!"

Corey put his dishes in the sink and asked if he could go to the condo pool. "Absolutely!" I said, "Have fun, Mr. Florian."

Allana said, "They have towels at the pool and the gym, no need to bring."

"Okay, mom."

Amidst chaos and countless obstacles, Victor had raised a damned fine young man.

NPR was still on. Allana snapped her fingers and pointed to her ear. We stared at each other as the commentator explained more about the deadly accident on the Brooklyn-

Queens Expressway. "Stuart 'Pinky' Goldstone, billionaire CEO of Goldstone Technologies Group, suffered a massive brain injury and died at the scene."

What the hell was Pinky doing on the BQE at 2 a.m.? His car was so severely crushed that it took a fire department rescue squad three hours to extricate his body from his beloved McLaren 650S. According to witnesses, a black Chevy Camaro might have been responsible for the accident. The McLaren drove straight into the base of a concrete overpass. The Camaro drove off without stopping. Allana insisted this was a professional hit executed by an experienced assassin. First, she ruled out the possibility of a high-speed PIT maneuver.

"Do you know what a PIT maneuver is, Ray?"

"Guess not."

"PIT stands for precision immobilization technique. It's a police tactic designed to stop fleeing cars. It was adapted from the bump and run technique used in stock car racing. But, if a PIT was used, Pinky's McLaren would have slowed and spun backward into the overpass."

"Yeah, I've seen that on TV, didn't know what it was called. How the hell do you know so much about it?"

"I was a morbid teenager. I wanted to be a blood splatter analyst." My eyes opened wide and Allana said, "Don't roll your eyes!"

"I'm not rolling anything, just had an involuntary ocular event."

"I majored in criminal justice before switching to visual studies. Guess I was always interested in all things involving visuality and forensics."

"Don't you think you should have told me about the blood splatter thing before we shacked up together?" Her viridian lasers burned. "Just kidding," I said. She laughed.

"My guess is, the Camaro forced pinky out of his lane and into the abutment at a speed approaching 100 miles per hour," said Allana.

The old girl seemed to know a lot about police procedure. What can I say? She was probably right about the accident, but for the sake of my blood pressure, I'd been trying *not* to think about Pinky, *and* ever since Victor died, I was doing everything possible to disengage with all things NoLab. The whole affair, I thought, had ended, vanished in a puff of smoke. Now, it seems, to have rematerialized in a ghoulish form. Was it just an unlucky accident, or a professional hit as Allana believed? And— what now?

***

Kaylee texted, "Urgent. Can we meet? Need to talk."

I responded, "Sure, but not at my apartment."

"And we can't meet at our place 'cause we're no longer there. On the lam. Crashing here and there. Remember your ex-grad student who made big fluorescent monochromes?"

"Yes."

"She hasn't moved since grad school. Still making the same paintings! Let's meet at her studio, Okay?"

"Okay. When?"

"Can you get there in an hour?"

"I can, but are you sure you want to meet? The last time we spoke it ended with you yelling 'fuck you' and then hanging up on me."

"Yeah, sorry, Ray—we still want to meet."

"Who's we?"

"Just Dave and me."

"What about Jeff?"

"He's gone…and out of control."

"See you in an hour."

"Sorry about Victor."

***

My beat up Toyota pickup truck was parked nearby. Used mostly for studio materials, but good to know it's there when the need to escape catastrophe might present itself.

Bushwick was an easy drive; I decided against taking the BQE. I knew who Kaylee was referring to—Maxine Shimomura, and I knew why she didn't mention her name and address over the phone.

Maxine's paintings are unforgettable—gigantic

monochromes in straight-out-of-the jar fluorescent colors. No images. No forms. Each painting is a field of pure unmodulated color. If you like flavor, you like Maxine's paintings. They're all flavor, nothing but flavor. What were those spicy cinnamon-ball candies called? Fireballs? Atomic Fireballs! Maxine's paintings were retina roasting Atomic Fireballs. One big dumb sensation, that's all, that's it, but what a kick and what relief from all the overworked, overthought, try-too-hard paintings in the world.

While I was driving, I got a call from Grace Germain. "It's about Madison Clark," she said. "He's dead. Had a massive heart attack last night." My first tendency was to raise my arms and shout "hallelujah," but no, I had to keep my hands on the wheel. Had to keep in lane. I hoped the Madison case would never materialize. Grace never thought it would—statute of limitations, Madison's many bad habits. Truth is, most collectors who purchased my pill pieces never actually ingested them—they're collectors for God's sake—and now they're happy cause those little pills, expired ingredients notwithstanding, are worth quite a lot. But, crazy Madison actually popped many. The news of his death was an enormous relief. I was floating. "Goodbye Grace, I love you!"

I had no trouble finding the building; it housed a garage with a homemade *flats fixed* sign, just as it did when Maxine was a student. I rang and got buzzed in, climbed the stairs to the fourth floor. The door opened before I knocked.

Kaylee greeted me with a hug—hmm. I shook hands with Dave and got a kind of awkward half-embrace, basically a shoulder bump, still—an unexpected gesture from such a painfully reserved young man. We sat in Maxine's studio, dwarfed by looming rectangles of yellow-green, hot pink, and fiery orange. Kaylee was dressed conservatively, a blue shirt and black slacks, a world away from the artfully ripped jeans and fuzzy-turtle-backpack she wore when we first met.

Kaylee spoke first, "Thanks for coming over, Ray. I'm sure you've heard about Pinky."

"Yes, on the news. So awful."

"It wasn't an accident you know."

"I don't know that for a fact, but it crossed my mind. Are you in trouble?"

"I guess you could say that," said Dave.

"We're staying in friends' apartments and studios. We move from place to place like Salman Rushdie for Christ's sake."

"And using burners," said Dave.

"We're fucked."

"What about Jeff?" I said.

"Jeff's the fucking problem," said Kaylee. "He's gone totally paranoid-schizo."

"So, what are you going to do? And, why am I here?"

"We don't know what to do, we're so fucked! *Fucked! Fucked! So—Fucked!*" Kaylee screamed.

Dave pulled Kaylee down to the couch and put his arms around her; he said to me, "We're hoping you could help us think this through. Other than Jeff, Kaylee and me, you're the only person left who knows us and the whole story, and—you're rational. We're a mess."

"Well, if you think Pinky was murdered, who do you think might have done it?" I said.

"At this point, so many people know we hacked their emails that it could be anybody or many anybodies," said Kaylee. Dave offered a beer. I could have used something stronger, but beer would do. Kaylee continued, "Yeah, and there are hundreds and hundreds of folks in those emails who we didn't target—innocent bystanders, so to speak—who are also in danger of being exposed, so now, you know, there are lots of suspects."

"You know, it *could* just have been a road rage accident, totally unrelated to NoLab. I really can't believe Pinky was killed to warn you not to release the emails. That would be some kind of insanely extreme warning, don't you think?"

"Yeah, some fucking crazy shit," said Kaylee. "Normal people don't do warnings like that, they say *they'll sue you* or *I'll call the cops.* They don't kill someone's father."

"Hey, this is what I urge you to do: Number one—do not post the hacked emails. Two—broadcast the fact that you will not release the information you have. Say it's been destroyed. And finally—you must go to the police and tell them everything. Hacking emails is illegal. You could get jail time for felonies like computer fraud or identity theft, but that's really not your problem now—right now, if you're right about Pinky's death, the possibility of being killed is your problem."

"Yeah, but Jeff has the files too. He's gone and we can't control him. There's no telling what he's gonna do."

"More reason to go to the police."

"Go to the police or don't go to the police, we're fucked either way," said Dave.

"Perhaps, but if you go to the police you might not be fucked corpses," I said. "How long can you live like this?"

"This is bad, but if Jeff posts the emails…I can't even imagine the mayhem, the waves of destruction, and all who will go under, including us," said Kaylee.

Their situation was hopeless. I was overcome with the need to get out of the room, to free myself from the glow of Maxine's super-saturated monoliths that has, for me, during the course of our short discussion, transformed from delightful luminosity to throbbing radiation burn.

"That's all I've got. That's all I can offer. I've got to go. Stay safe," I said, and I bid them farewell with half-hearted embraces.

"Yeah, peace and love," said Jeff sarcastically.

Kaylee's face and welling tears were glowing fluorescent green. Leaving them like this was painful, but there was nothing I could do. I just had to get out of there.

15

The following day, I had two grad reviews to attend, semiannual opportunities to monitor the progress of individual grad students. Typically, they take place in the student's studio and are attended by the student-artist and a four-member faculty review committee. First up was a grad who made short digital films utilizing a single original source—the movie *Chinatown*. As odd and restrictive as this may sound, she made around a dozen films, all from the footage of this single movie. She said she could spend her entire life rearranging the frames of *Chinatown* and never lose interest or repeat herself. Working with her was a total pleasure. Most of the Profs on her committee were supportive, more because she was articulate and she worked her ass off than because they liked or understood what she was up to.

The second review was painful. I was not this student's official committee member—I would never agree to serve on a committee like this—I was just sitting in for a colleague who couldn't attend. The paintings were derivative messes. The student had no idea why he was painting these things. Didn't know the history of what he was doing. I told him, "You can't make a good painting by simply putting in everything you like. It's just not that easy. You like ice cream and steak and peanut butter and sushi— but if you throw them all in a pot and cook'em, it'll taste like shit. You can't make your paintings better by throwing in more things you like—that's just a self-indulgent fantasy." The student's face was vacant. Why did I bother? Trying to be a good temporary committee member I guess, not the prof with the bad attitude. And, if you really want to know, at this point in my teaching career I was tired of having to make and defend value judgments. I was ready to join good old Pope Francis—as in—"Who am I to judge?" I just want to work with the smartest grads and watch them do crazy things. If one of them was so insecure as to ask me which way to proceed, I now resolved to say things like—*Listen to the wind in the trees. Follow the water in the brook.*

***

After the reviews, I was feeling kind of lost, and there was no Victor to bounce off. As I left Watson Hall, a wiry guy in an iridescent blue suit and wraparound sunglasses approached. He introduced himself as Detective Kazmarek and flashed his shield. Rubbing his bald head, he said, "Professor Lawson, can I ask you a few questions?"

"Of course, sure, but just call me Ray, please. I hate that

Professor stuff."

"Mind if we sit down here?" He motioned to a low brick wall at the edge of the path.

"I assume you heard about the death of Stuart Goldstone."

"Yes, I heard it on the news."

"What was your relationship to Mr. Goldstone?"

"Wow. That's a long, complex story. Do you really want to hear it all?"

"For now, just paint me a rough picture."

"Well, many years ago, here at Columbia, I was the teacher of Stuart Goldstone's son Jeffery.

"When was that?"

"Around 2001."

"Go on."

"Well, since Jeff graduated, I followed his career. I'd run into him and occasionally Stuart at various art events. I didn't really know Stuart—I mean we weren't friends. We never socialized or anything. We existed in completely different worlds. Then in August, out of the blue, Stuart called me to say Jeff was missing, and asked if I could help find him. That's my relationship in a nutshell."

"Why didn't he go to the police if his son went missing?"

"Good question. I asked him that myself. He said he wanted to keep it all confidential."

"When was the last time you saw Stuart Goldstone?"

Around a month ago. I can check my calendar later if

you need to know the exact exact date."

"Did he tell you anything about being threatened? Did he have any enemies?"

"I had the impression he had many enemies, Peter Rademacher for one. He's the CEO of Anatolean Worldwide. You might find this interesting, Detective—the very last moment I saw Stuart he was running from a drone in Central Park."

Rubbing his head, Detective Kazmarek said, "I'll be damned. So, what do you know about the drone?"

"It had a video camera attached, and I saw it chase him."

"A freaking drone. That's a new one!"

"So, I'm assuming you don't think his death was an accident."

"Do you?"

"I'm not really sure."

My phone pinged a text alert. "Emergency," from Kaylee, "Call me." Then another ping, this one from Allana, "Call Kaylee."

"Detective Kazmarek, I need to make an important call."

"Are you able to come to the station tomorrow and answer more questions?"

"I can do that."

"The FBI is also interested in this case. Okay with you if an agent joins in?"

"That's okay. Why are they involved?"

"They're looking at the wider case."

NoLab

He rubbed his head briskly a few times front to back and gave me his card. We decided on a time to meet.

***

As I walked downtown on Broadway, I phoned Kaylee. She was breathless. "Jeff's streaming live on Facebook right now!" I found a bench on the median, sat down and *tuned in*, if that's how you say it. After a few screw-ups, I found Jeff's stream. There he was, plain as day, standing someplace that looked like a hotel or apartment balcony. Behind the balcony—the ocean and palm trees. Jeff looked *out of it*. He was pacing, gesticulating, ranting: "…is so very ugly. I'm sick and tired of the corruption. The lying, the profiteering. This is an artwork, but not one to decorate your bourgeois wall. This one has use-value. It's a work of NoLab, but I'm all that's left of NoLab. Now, I am NoLab. In the spirit of Hans Haacke's *Real-Time Social System* of 1971, NoLab, A.K.A. Jeffry W. Goldstone is hereby launching a digital artwork titled *Ten*. Lots of people don't want me to release these emails—so-called friends, the United States Government, Dia, even Dia. Many corrupt individuals and corporations have conspired to stop the release of these emails. Well, fuck them! Peter Rademacher, CEO of Anatolian Worldwide, killed my father to prevent the completion of this artwork. He thinks that'll scare me off. Fuck Rademacher!" Now whispering, Jeff continued,

"Hey, art world, stick your pretty paintings up your ass. They killed Lombardi, ya know. He was right about the shadow network, dead right! Banking—arms—oil—cocaine—D.C.—Riyadh—London. Suicide, my ass!"

Jeff grabbed a laptop, held it up and displayed its screen for the camera. "Now I'm officially releasing *Ten*." On my cell phone, I could clearly see Jeff's fingers on the computer keyboard and a folder labeled TEN silently slide across the screen to an uploading dock. Jeff spoke again, "It's done! It's in the world! *Ten* is now complete. It's an artwork that'll actually *do* something! The underbelly of the art world is now on display. Dummy corporations, money laundering, tax evasion, fraud—it's all here for your viewing pleasure. It's Byzantine…hey…"

Jeff was abruptly knocked to the ground. There were shouts, *"Mira! El computadora! Conseguir el computadora!"* About a half-dozen guys, clearly some kind of SWAT team or black ops unit, were shoving furniture around. Two had Jeff on the floor, face down. They bound his hands behind his back with plastic ties. One grabbed the laptop and smashed it on the edge of the railing.

Sitting on a bench in the Broadway median where people usually chat with friends, or rest with their shopping bags, or read *La Voz Hispana*, I stared at the little screen of my phone, witnessing a crime unfolding somewhere very far away. The image jerked violently, zigzagged, turned upside down, and then went blank. Now I heard the car horns on

Broadway, children laughing, a deranged man shouting obscenities. A text came in. It was from Kaylee. "Shit! It's ALL online! Going underground. Wish us luck."

***

Instead of taking my usual subway ride home, I hailed a cab. It bumped and jerked its way to Brooklyn. Who were those guys in black? Probably not soldiers, and not an official police SWAT team. They wore no insignias, no badges. Some kind of private mercenaries no doubt. And where exactly did this all take place? My guess, South America or the Caribbean. Jeff was smart. He would have gone to a country that didn't share extradition with the U.S. Bet he thought he was sitting pretty. I wondered if we'd ever hear from him again, and would we ever know who arranged for him to vanish. The perpetrators' intervention was in vain. Before the computer was destroyed, the emails went online for all to see. What could have been so important in those hacked emails that could warrant this kind of violence?

The cab dropped me off at my new concrete and glass residence. I took the elevator up. It pinged on every floor as an aid to the blind. What a thoughtful touch. A caring machine. It made you feel decent, civilized. Hadn't lived in a building with an elevator since Fourth Street. There, back then, every tenant had to take turns running the building's old industrial elevator. It was a big manual job with a sliding gate, so, you know, you could see the walls of the shaft go by. The tenants got to know each other well. For years the building was quiet and easy, mostly artists and dancers, but as the seventies wore on, and the rents went up, new people moved in and started private clubs and disco nights. Eventually, a couple of women from California turned the third floor into a primal scream therapy workshop. Conservative looking, middle-aged men with business suits and attaché cases showed up. Adult diapers were delivered. Sometimes, when on elevator duty, we'd hear screaming and stop the car near three to eavesdrop. *Primal* was about right. Piercing, heartbreaking screams and shouts, and cries of "mommy, mommy" reverberated up and down the elevator shaft. Since then, I hear those screams in every elevator I enter.

Ping! The elevator door opened. When I entered the apartment, Becher ran toward me, panting. He sniffed my cuffs as I poured some vodka, threw in ice, sat down and turned on CNN. I really needed a drink. Today, dear Becher would have to wait a few extra minutes to pee.

Allana came home with Thai food, saw the state I was in and without saying a word took Becher out for his walk. She's a saint. We took our chopsticks out of their paper sleeves and pulled them apart like wishbones, ate pad thai out of the containers, CNN droning on. Allana knew something was up, after all, she alerted me to Kaylee's text.

She listened to my tale of woe: my discussion with Detective Kazmarek, and what I saw on Jeff's deranged live-stream rant. I also told her I had an appointment to speak to the police and the FBI the following day.

"Ray, you should consider getting a lawyer to help you navigate what is becoming a hazardous obstacle course."

"I *have* a lawyer—Grace Germain."

"So, speak to her. Okay, darling?" We kissed and she went upstairs to read before bed. I nursed my vodka and, with CNN on in the background, began to sort through papers from Victor's loft.

Victor's brain overflowed. Some ideas were brilliant, some just nuts. There was no separation between his life and his art. Whatever Victor did or thought just entered the stream; everything flowed together. He made lists, observations, proposals, collections. The files were in disarray. The cardboard boxes bulged.

The carton I looked through that evening was full of quotations—quotations ripped from newspapers, Xeroxed from books, and handwritten by Victor. Here's a selection:

My friends are wondering why did I watch Anna Nicole Smith's show. Why do I watch WrestleMania? My answer is…the poet must not avert his eyes…

- Werner Herzog

And most important, before I knew what art was I was an ironmonger.

- David Smith

If it sounds good it is good.
- Duke Ellington

You know more than you think you do.
- Dr. Spock, first sentence of *Baby and Child Care*

I woke up one day and everything in the apartment had been stolen and replaced with an exact replica. I said to my roommate, "Can you believe this? Everything in the apartment has been stolen and replaced with an exact replica." He said, "Do I know you?"
- Steven Wright

A musical instrument is a mysterious thing, inhabiting a complex sort of space: it is both an ordinary three-dimensional object and a portal to another world; it exists as a physical entity solely so that it—and, indeed, physicality—can be transcended.
- Joyce Carol Oates

I like museums. I like to look out of their windows.
- Gertrude Stein

Culture is the refinement which belongs to gentlemen, art is the raw stuff.
- David Smith

NoLab

From a handbill, at First Avenue between 9th and 10th Streets, for a musical combo called The Backyards, *looking for a drummer: "Must be dedicated, hard-hitting, in it for life. Willing to die naked in an alley for your anti-art. Outcasts and social rejects preferred but not essential."*

And as Henry Geldzahler, a former Commissioner of Cultural Affairs for New York City, tells it, he rejected the first portrait Andy Warhol made of him—as a gift—in the early 1970's. "I told him, 'This is nothing but a Polaroid with silk-screen added. You left out the art,' Andy said, 'I knew I forgot something.'"
- Grace Glueck

Woman to Rauschenberg—*"My child could do that."*
Rauschenberg—*"But Madam, day after day after day?"*

As I read my way through Victor's papers, a small stack of photos slipped out and fell to the floor. It nearly hit poor Becher who jumped up and out of his slumber. I rubbed his head, picked up the photos, removed the brittle rubber band, and leafed through the yellowed black and white snapshots.

- Baby Corey sitting on Victor's lap. They are on the front steps of a brick apartment building. Brooklyn? Corey is wearing a diaper and a striped t-shirt; he appears to be about six months old. Victor is wearing a dark short-sleeved shirt with three white diamonds down the right side. He is laughing and holding a cigar; he looks so young.

- Victor in Vietnam with two buddies, all three in camo, holding their M16 rifles in mock shooting poses.

- Victor and his first wife, Elise, at the beach. They are wearing bathing suits. Victor is clowning, flexing a bicep. On a blanket, Elise is posing glam in an ironic sort of way. It looks like they're at Coney Island.

- Victor and Elise at their wedding.

- Corey, maybe three, wearing an ornate cowboy shirt, cowboy boots, and a holster with a toy pistol. A cowboy hat hangs at his back from the cord around his neck. He isn't smiling. He holds Elise's hand. Other children are present. Perhaps they're at a party. Elise is quite beautiful in a turtleneck sweater and slacks. She is squinting, her face sullen.

I couldn't go on looking at the photos, too painful. Just need to finish the quotations.

I remember my work, not word for word, to be sure, but in some more accurate, trustworthy way; my whole work has come to resemble a terrain of which I have made a thorough, geodetic survey, not from a desk, with pen and ruler, but by touch, by getting down on all fours, on my stomach, and crawling over the ground inch by inch, and this over an endless period of time in all conditions of weather.

- Henry Miller

Generally, art wavers between being closer to a book or closer to a rug—more conceptual or more decorative. Our work is somewhere in between. We try to make conceptual rugs.

- Vitaly Komar

On the work of Komar & Melamid

In the sixties, however, I felt like a dog looking at a forest, seeing countless trees and thinking, "So little time, so much to do!" Now we're down to one tree that hundreds of dogs have already pissed on.

- John Baldessari

Don't let yourself become hypnotized by the smiles of yesterday; rather invent the smiles of tomorrow.

- Henri-Piere Roche, 1953

...all conservatism is based upon the idea that if you leave things alone you leave them as they are. But you do not. If you leave a thing alone, you leave it to a torrent of change. If you leave a white post alone it will soon be a black post. If you particularly want it to be white, you must be always painting it again; that is, you must be always having a revolution. Briefly, if you want the old white post you must have a new white post. But this which is true even of inanimate things is in a quite special and terrible sense true of all human things.

- Gilbert K. Chesterton

(At the top of this quotation, Victor wrote the word "yes" in big block letters.)

One cannot understand Dada; one must experience it. Dada is immediate and obvious. If you're alive, you are a Dadaist.

  - Richard Huelsenbeck

You are only as original as the obscurity of your sources.

  - David Pease

Writing shit about new snow
for the rich
is not art.

  - Kobayashi Issa 1763-1827 - Japan

What tiresome and laborious folly it is to write lengthy tomes, to expound in five hundred pages on an idea that one could easily propound orally in a few minutes. Better is pretending that the books exist already and offering a summary or commentary.

  - Jorge Luis Borges

Everything is mystery, ourselves, and all things both simple and humble.

  - Giorgio Morandi

It was about 1:00 a.m. when I came upon a folder labeled *Tabloid Fountain*. In 1999 Victor submitted a proposal for a sculpture competition sponsored by Storm King. I remembered it very well—it was freaking brilliant. I was extremely jealous, that's how I knew how good it was. I had to look at the proposal again. Damn the hour! *Tabloid Fountain* wasn't selected by the jury. Too real? Too tough? Whatever. In any case, Victor was cool with the outcome. He tossed away ideas that could sustain your run of the mill artist for a lifetime. Seeing this proposal again, after all these years, I knew one thing—this piece needed to be realized! Somewhere. Anywhere. It would kill at the lake in MacArthur Park, with the L.A skyline as a backdrop. Perhaps I'll make it my mission. Looking at the drawings, the documentation, and the photos of a sweet maquette constructed with a toy car and truck had me laughing and crying at once.

Tabloid Fountain, the proposal, specified that a white 1969 Lincoln Continental be suspended eight feet above the water at the edge of the lake at Storm King. The car was to be supported by straps in the customary manner of a tow-truck winch-raising a submerged vehicle. The Lincoln in its sling is suspended by a cable from the boom of a supremely industrial, chrome-laden, heavy-duty, red Kenworth tow-truck parked at the edge of the lake (a magnificent vehicle with a twenty-ton boom). Water is gushing from the Lincoln's undercarriage into the lake, creating a cascade that suggests the Lincoln has just then been hoisted from the water. It appears to be the scene of an accident. The viewer always and eternally arrives at the very moment the car has been raised. Water flows continuously. It's a goddamned fountain! The trick is obvious—water is pumped from the lake, up the tow-truck boom, down along the cable supporting the car, and into the undercarriage where it then cascades to the lake—an endless loop. Evading the plague of insipid public sculptures, *Tabloid Fountain* would be a fountain for our time! A permanent crime scene. An eternal accident. Yes, it should definitely be sited in L.A., the epicenter of vehicular death, catapulting crashes, drive-bys, marathon chases, and Sig alerts.

I fell asleep with a Kenworth wrecker catalog on my chest, the television on. At 3:00 a.m. I woke to a news alert. "In a bizarre chain of events, Jeffrey Goldstone, son of recently deceased billionaire Stuart Goldstone, was apparently kidnapped in Cuba during a live-stream broadcast during which he released hacked emails." National TV! Jesus Christ! The magnitude of the NoLab hacking was really sinking in. How did I ever allow my self to be sucked into this bottomless hellhole?

16

The next morning at breakfast, Allana reminded me that Corey was coming over Saturday, and—he was bringing a date! After Allana left for work, I called Grace. I explained as much as I could in our brief phone conversation and told her I was scheduled to meet with the police and the FBI. Basically, she agreed with Allana, I needed a lawyer, and in Grace's own words, "someone more high-powered than me." She recommended Andrew Coleman, a criminal defense attorney at Mason, Coleman, and McQueen. She would make arrangements.

"Cancel your meeting today, and reschedule when Andrew can accompany you," she advised.

"It's okay, I didn't do anything illegal. I'll do the meeting today. Don't worry."

"That's not smart, Ray."

"Don't worry, Grace."

"Well, if you go alone, make your answers as short as possible and do not answer any question with more information than requested. Do NOT volunteer ANYTHING."

***

I can't say what Grace might have thought about my conduct at the 19th Precinct. Detective Kazmarek was there, a very pregnant FBI agent, and even someone from Homeland Security. Couldn't help realize how serious this investigation was and how treacherous the terrain. Detective Kazmarek began, "A lot has changed since we talked, eh?"

"Sadly, yes."

"Thought we were just investigating Stuart Goldstone's death, now we've got illegal hacking and his son Jeff's apparent abduction in Cuba—jeez."

I was asked to start at the beginning and simply tell them what I knew and what my role was. I told them the story, from the time Pinky first approached me in the dark hall of my building to Jeff's live-stream release of the hacked emails and his violent abduction. I never lied, except by omission. Didn't say anything about the incident with the biker thugs—no one asked. I failed to mention the Institute, because now it seemed irrelevant. The FBI agent was fixated on learning where Dave and Kaylee were, but *that* I didn't know. She asked, "What does email hacking have to do with art? That's what I don't get. Were there any pictures stolen or what?"

"No, no paintings were involved. Whoever said art was

involved was most likely referring to conceptual art, not traditional painting and sculpture."

"Conceptual art?"

"Okay—conceptual art is art that is generally concerned with ideas. It relates to objects *only* as they might pertain to ideas."

"So how do the hacked emails relate to this conceptual art?"

"Well, NoLab, as an artists' collective, simply claimed the project to be a work of conceptual art. They could have called the release of the hacked emails political action or whistleblowing, and the legal system undoubtedly knows it as computer fraud, but NoLab chose to see it in the tradition of activist art interventions and so—it's a work of art. They intended to expose the hidden workings of the art establishment. Institutional Critique. A kind of meta-project."

"Meta-project?"

"Well…"

"Never mind. To us, they're just felons."

***

Saturday afternoon Allana and I prepared dinner for Cory and his date. We agreed to grill veggie burgers, brats, and corn, so, aside from making guacamole and cleaning up, there wasn't much to do. CNN was blasting. It was the new soundtrack of my life. Radio or TV news was always on now. Needed to keep up with the ongoing consequences of Jeff's release of the hacked emails, *and*, despite my best effort to resist, I was developing a masochistic compulsion to track Trump's every insane utterance and to scrutinize its destructive impact. On both fronts it had been one calamity after another. The intercom rang. We buzzed Corey in. He seemed a bit embarrassed when Allana gave him a big hug, and I think she sensed it too and proceeded to enthusiastically hug his date to kind of make extreme hugging appear to be her standard greeting. I decided to go with just shaking hands. Little Becher ran around excitedly, sliding on the travertine floor, tail whipping—Corey and his friend giggled.

We put out the guacamole and offered drinks; they asked for Cokes. Since Corey made no introduction, I said, "So, Corey, who is your friend?"

"Um, this is Fran."

"Hi, Fran. I'm Ray."

"And my name's Allana. We're so glad to meet you."

Fran shyly nodded her acknowledgment.

"Hope you guys like brats and veggie burgers."

"Brats, mmm good," said Corey.

"Ray, do you have an iPad?" Corey asked.

"Yes I do, sir."

"Could we borrow it? The one dad got me, broke."

"Sure, I hardly ever use it. So, take it home and keep it as long as you want. It's just collecting dust here."

"Thanks, Ray! We're gonna play *Hackycat.*"

Allana said, "Dinner should be ready in about an hour. Just help yourself to more Cokes or anything else in the fridge, okay?"

As Corey replied, "Okay, thank you," Becher, standing stone-still with legs spread wide on the kitchen floor, began to pee. Fran and Corey found this hysterically funny. It seemed impossible that such a small dog could be the vessel for all that liquid. As yellow rivulets broke off from the main pool and meandered off erratically in many directions, Allana and I laughed too. As I mopped up, I made a mental note: gotta remember, the excited dog bladder is a dangerous thing.

I grilled the dinner out on the balcony and we all gathered around the dining room table for a family meal. Fran was a sweet young woman. She too had Down syndrome.

"So where did you two meet?" asked Allana.

"At work," said Corey.

"We eat lunch together. Corey always saves a chair for me. He's my friend," Fran said loudly and rapidly.

"Fran's the prettiest girl at work," said Corey. Fran smiled.

"What do your parents do?" Said Allana.

"They're divorced. My mom's a doctor. She's funny. I never see my dad. He used to come around, but not anymore."

"What kind of doctor?" Allana asked.

"A baby doctor. A pediatrician. She works at New York Presba...New York Presbaterium...darn, I always have trouble saying that."

"Yes, New York-Presbyterian—you got it fine. That's an excellent hospital, your mom must be a very good doctor," said Allana.

Looking at Fran, Corey said, "I bet Ray asks you what you think about Trump."

"Now why do you say that?" I said.

"You ask everyone."

"Really. Hm. I never noticed. So, Fran, what's your opinion of our President?"

Corey shouted, "I told you!"

"I don't like him. My mom says he's mean," said Fran.

"My dad used to say Trump was an a-hole," said Corey, "and Ray says…"

"Enough talk about politics," said Allana. "How about helping me clear the table so we can have gelato."

"Yeah," said Corey.

Fran and Corey removed the dishes and set the table for dessert. Allana gave me instructions on proper topics for the occasion. We ate our gelato and chatted about light and pleasant things until Corey said, "Dad would like to be here. He'd like this gelato. He'd like telling you jokes." Allana looked at me and nodded, a sign I interpreted as, *let*

Corey go on, let him get it off his chest.

"I miss my dad. I'm sorry that he isn't in the world enjoying his life anymore. Dad treated me like a real person. He treated me nice. He thought I was cool. So…I think…I think that part of me…that *me* that feels good about myself, that *me* that can feel like a regular normal person sometimes, I think *that* died with my dad. Everyone else looks at me like I'm a freak. That's all they see, so that's what I am."

Allana immediately got up and walked to Corey and embraced him. I saw the tears in her eyes. She bravely kept from completely losing it. Fran got up and joined in. I was choked up too, so, what the hell, I got in on the group hug. Becher wasn't one to be left out; he was right there licking Fran's legs. Allana said, "Corey, everyone in this room and so many others know you are absolutely awesome. Please never forget that."

***

After Corey and Fran departed, Allana and I cleaned up. When we finished, Allana turned toward me and looked into my eyes. We instinctively grabbed each other and embraced. We just stood there, in the middle of the kitchen, sobbing in each other's arms. Allana and I let it all out.

When we separated, Allana went off to rinse her face;

she returned with two glasses of Mezcal Vago. We sat and talked about the evening. "Fran's a good kid. They're such a cute couple," said Allana.

"Yeah, but any kind of relationship will be a complicated transaction for them. They crave independence, but they are mired in dependency."

"They face so many obstacles. It's really unbearable," said Allana.

"Corey's such decent young man…the abuse he has to endure…yes, it's unbearable. I'm surprised Victor never killed anyone in Corey's defense. You know, Corey's character might just be Victor's greatest achievement. Victor did good. Fucking good. I had no idea. I'm ashamed."

"Now *we're* here to watch over him," said Allana.

"It's no accident. It was Victor's plan."

"He was a real father till the very end."

"Allana, don't you think Corey has something deep going on? He said some profound things about death today. When he was talking, the cliché, 'still water runs deep,' came to mind. Is that demeaning?"

"No, no, I don't think so. Something like that occurred to me too, like Archilochus's saying—'The fox knows many things, but the hedgehog knows one big thing'," said Allana.

"I thought Isaiah Berlin said that."

"No, he expanded on the idea, but the Greeks got there

first." Allana raised her glass and said, "Here's to our magnificent Corey."

"To Cor," I said.

Allana went upstairs to bed. She's sensible; I poured more mezcal and turned on CNN. Jake Tapper had an update on the release of the NoLab emails and Jeff's kidnapping. He announced that no ransom requests had been received and no contact had yet been made by the kidnappers, and for the first time in the media, Stuart Goldstone's death was mentioned in connection with NoLab, Jeff, and the hacked emails. As Tapper saw it, "It was a bizarre kidnapping...preceded by the death of Jeffrey Goldstone's father in a suspicious hit and run accident... was it more than a coincidence?" CNN proceeded to air the very same live-stream video I viewed on my cell phone while sitting alone on a bench in the Broadway median. It was more painful to watch the second time around. Jeff ranting. Jeff accusing Peter Rademacher of the death of his father. Jeff releasing the cache of hacked emails. Jeff thrown to the ground, hands tied, computer destroyed. The only good thing I could say about the whole sad incident was—Jeff didn't mention Victor or me.

17

The next morning, early, I leashed up little Becher and headed out for our morning walk. I'm not superstitious, but I've come to believe that, somehow, Victor's spirit had entered Becher. I mean, really. Becher *was* Victor now. Like Victor, the hairy little mutt did everything *all out*, full throttle, no hesitation. Becher's got Victor's childlike enthusiasm for everything. And, do I need to mention the anal fixation?

Becher peed on the first lamppost we came to. A coffee vendor was setting up on the sidewalk in the dark. I picked up a *New York Times* from a corner kiosk. Just delivered, the papers sat bundled on the ground. The proprietor had to clip the binding to get my copy.

I found a fire hydrant that protruded from the side of a building, a stately double-headed unit with chains looping down from hexagonal caps like twin watch fobs, and there I sat, beneath the light from a Napa auto parts sign, in my grungy urban study. Becher delighted in all the glorious fragrances the Brooklyn sidewalk had to offer.

On the front page:

"Artist Releases Hacked Emails: Abducted by Unknown Assailants in Havana." By Ralph M. Easton.

December 8, 2016. Jeffrey Goldstone, 41, an artist and member of the art collaborative NoLab, released hacked emails while live streaming a disjointed rant from the balcony of the Bravo Del Este Hotel in Havana, Cuba. The Facebook Livestream ended in a bizarre abduction in which Mr. Goldstone was violently manhandled by six masked men clad in black SWAT gear. His computer was targeted and destroyed.

Jeffrey Goldstone is the son of the recently deceased billionaire Stuart Goldstone who died one week earlier on December 2nd in an early morning accident on the Brooklyn-Queens Expressway. Another car is thought to have been involved; the driver has not been identified.

Because the release of the hacked emails is ensnaring many prominent public and private figures in an expanding web of alleged illicit activities, the New York Police Department, the FBI, and Homeland Security are establishing a joint task force.

NoLab was established in 2001 by Jeffrey Goldstone, Kaylee Boone, and Dave Collins. It is known for its public art projects and interventions of a conceptual nature. During its fifteen-year history, additional artists, designers, and technicians have participated in NoLab projects; some became members for extended periods, most notably, the artist/tech entrepreneur Lyonel Whitfield. His involvement with NoLab ended in 2012.

Ten, *the artwork Mr. Goldstone referred to in his live stream, is a self-described conceptual project intended to track the finances of today's ten wealthiest art world players.* Ten *was meant to revisit* *Hans Haacke's controversial artwork,* Shapolsky et al. Manhattan Real Estate Holdings, a Real-Time Social System, as of May 1, 1971. Shapolsky et al…*was primarily documentation of the transactions and holdings of the Shapolsky real estate empire that included large tracts of slum housing in New York City. A network of dummy corporations and family ties obscured its holdings.* Shapolsky et al…*was scheduled for a 1971 exhibition at the Guggenheim Museum. At the time, there was speculation that some Guggenheim board members were connected to the real estate group, but it remained conjecture. The Guggenheim canceled the Haacke exhibition six weeks before it was scheduled to open.*

February 2015, Dia:Beacon received a substantial gift to commission new work for a five-year programming series featuring activist art and design collectives. NoLab was one of the recipient collectives funded and was scheduled for a solo exhibition at Dia:Beacon late 2017. On September 13, 2016, however, Dia:Beacon publicly announced that its anonymous benefactor withdrew support. Dia canceled the entire series.

Detective Tadeusz Kazmarek, NYPD, 19th precinct, in a recently released statement, discussed aspects of the ongoing investigation: "NoLab members were aware that hacking emails and releasing hacked emails could subject them to criminal liability. Ironically, they became victims themselves. They were harassed and threatened by individuals and corporations attempting to prevent them from making the hacked email public. The NYPD is also considering the relationship of NoLab's email hack to the death last week of Stuart

Goldstone, Jeffrey Goldstone's father. Stuart Goldstone hired Columbia University Professors Ray Lawson and Victor Florian to find NoLab when the three members originally went missing."

Professor Nathan Cruz, a cybersecurity expert and Director of the Center for Computer Security at the Hayes Institute in Ann Arbor, told the Times: "This NoLab group used some sophisticated key mapping tools to break passwords. But primarily they employed the most common and primitive, but extremely effective hacking method: spear phishing. Phishers basically send messages to their selected victims through social media. Some of these messages might appear to be sent by friends via Twitter or Facebook. Invitations to private exhibitions, unique investment opportunities, or exclusive vacations, for example. When the links are clicked, malicious files infect the targeted networks.

"As far as we know at this moment, over ten thousand emails and attachments were involved in the released cache. That's roughly 16,000 pages of documents from the last four years. Most were from secondary or tertiary sources."

Washington Post *reporter, Kim Ashby, said on* Face the Nation, Sunday: *"The hacked material we looked at was not redacted. Many innocent people, folks who were in the wrong place at the wrong time, will be injured by the Goldstone release. Many individuals and corporations have had or will have criminal activities exposed—I should say alleged criminal activities. The most newsworthy items we've seen so far involve the business transactions of Peter Rademacher, the CEO of the I.T. firm, Anatolian Worldwide. The Goldstone emails we looked at contain long chains that appear to implicate Rademacher and Anatolian in an extensive money-laundering scheme. A multi-national investigation is already being discussed. It is expected that dozens of powerful people and global corporations will be yanked up and into the media spotlight.*

"We're all reading through the transcripts as fast as we can. I expect you'll be seeing a lot more heads roll in the coming weeks."

- Excerpts from the complete transcript of the Goldstone emails and the entire live-stream video are available online.

Becher started whimpering. We found a patch of grass around a dying tree and the little guy did his business.

***

After the *Times* article, there was a daily succession of reports featuring corruption exposed by the Goldstone emails—corporate greed, cover-ups, fraud, money laundering. Additionally, the ten top art world investors, whose emails NoLab hacked, had business associates, casual acquaintances, friends, family, and lovers. All their private emails to-and-from "the ten" also entered the public domain. It was as if NoLab was one of those hapless thieves who steals a car, unaware that there's a baby in the backseat. The hacked Goldstone documents were released intermittently, as fast as the media could separate items of significance from the reams of chatter.

Peter Rademacher's problems multiplied. He and

Anatolian were entangled, along with a few celebrities, in a Malaysian embezzlement scandal involving billion-dollar transactions and illegal investments in art, yachts, and real estate.

Tobacco Heiress Margaret "Midge" Cartwright purchased ancient Iraqi artifacts intended as gifts to the Metropolitan Museum of Art. Emails to the antiquities dealer in Jerusalem who arranged the transactions revealed that both Ms. Cartwright and the dealer were quite aware that the artifacts were looted; in fact, they were obtained illegally by ISIS militants.

***

Since Pinky's death, I've spent my days with the media as they churned out news about NoLab and the rise of Trump. Two tragedies that will forever remain intertwined in my memory. The NoLab news hurt, but Trump's pronouncements were excruciating, and the fucker hasn't even been sworn in yet. I wonder, how long will it be and what will it take for all Americans to come to the realization that they've been screwed?

***

The following night I awoke to Allana's distressed face. She was pleading, "Ray, Ray, wake up. Ray, you were having a bad dream. You were shouting and flailing in your sleep."

"I'm so sorry. What time is it?"

"3 a.m."

"Jeez, so sorry. I had a horrendous nightmare. Incredibly vivid."

"Do you remember it?"

"Every detail. I'll never forget it."

"Then tell me. It'll be good to get it out."

"I don't want to freak you out."

"That's an impossibility, Luv."

"Okay, but it's pretty dark."

"Don't worry, please. First, let me get a towel to dry you off."

When she got back, I told Allana my nightmare exactly as remembered.

I was watching TV news. President Trump and a sports reporter from a local TV station were on the golf course at Mar-a-Lago. The reporter's name was Diane Spurlock. She was young, pretty, and blond. She wore a bright green polo shirt and pink Bermuda shorts. The occasion appeared to be a celebrity golf tournament. Wayne Newton, Gary Busey, Dennis Rodman, and Hulk Hogan were bantering with Trump. Trump turned to the reporter. The camera zoomed in on the two of them.

"Diane, we're raking in mega bucks for charity today, the sick kids and the nuns at Saint Francis are gonna have big smiles on their

faces, big smiles."

"This is so great."

"Right, right. Have you seen all the big celebrities here? Gary, the Hulk, Dennis, Wayne. Such big stars. Such big stars. Really big. Good people."

"Yes, it's so amazing to have them here!"

"They're not getting paid you know, they're here because Donald J. Trump invited them."

"Palm Beach County appreciates your generosity, Mr. Trump."

"Diane, delightful Diane, I want to talk about something important today, something very big. This is an exclusive story just for you."

"Wow! I'm honored! I'm sure our audience will want to hear all about it!"

"Do you know how many people die every year in the United States?"

"How many people die? No, Mr. Trump, sorry...no idea."

"Well, it's over two and one-half million people. Do you know what happens to the crowns and fillings when all these people die?"

"You mean like...fillings...in the mouth?"

"Yes, like in the mouth, sweetie."

"I imagine, people get buried with their dental work."

"Correct! They bury all that silver and gold...or the crooks that run the crematoriums steal it. Now don't you think that's a terrible waste?"

"I...I don't know. I never thought about it."

"No one's gonna rip off America while Donald Trump is

President. Do you know what gold is worth today?"

"Well, I know it's worth a lot."

To clarify the approximations I was about to make, I said to Allana, "Here, Trump said *something* like:"

"One thousand two hundred forty-three dollars and sixty-four cents an ounce. So, dear—you are such a doll. You know that? My first executive order—well, after the wall—will mandate the extraction of all silver and gold dental work from the dead. Those useless corpses will generate one hundred million dollars a year, one hundred million dollars that have been flushed down the toilet…till now. This executive order is gonna be a big win-win, believe me." He put his hand on the reporter's shoulder and massaged her deltoid. Then Trump said, "Can't believe no one's thought of this before." The poor, confused reporter stared into the camera.

"That's it, I said."

Allana shuddered, and said, "That *was* a nasty dream. The scariest part is that it's all too close to reality."

Allana kissed my forehead, and we did our best to grab a little sleep.

18

In the morning we slowly made our way to the kitchen. "You okay now, Ray?"

"I don't think I'll ever be okay. But, yeah, sure, I'm fine."

"I think you should curtail your media fixation. Too much MSNBC, CNN, and NPR, babe. That was a media-overload nightmare. Never heard a dream like that before. Are we all gonna be dreaming in tweets now? Hmm, I expect there'll be many new categories in the *Diagnostic and Statistical Manual of Mental Disorders* dealing with Trump/media psychoses."

"I hear you loud and clear. And, thanks for being there for me."

Allana smiled and waved her arm as if to say *forget it.*

I watched Allana prepare her fruit and yogurt. I knew for sure, I was the luckiest man alive.

"That Trump is making the world uglier by the minute," said Allana.

"Yeah, and add Victor's death, Pinky's deadly accident, Jeff's abduction, Kaylee and Dave in hiding, and the never-ending fallout from the hacked emails—what more can go wrong?"

"Kaylee and Dave are in hiding? I didn't know that."

"No? Sorry, guess I forgot to tell you. So much has been happening."

"Where are they?"

"I have no idea. That's the big question, and that's what Detective Kazmarek and the FBI want to know too. Right after Jeff released the emails, I got a text from Kaylee saying they were going underground. That's all I know. Guess they assumed they'd be the ones to pay for Jeff's desperate act."

"Poor things."

"I'm feeling guilty about all this. Survivor guilt. I got Victor involved. Got all of us involved, really. And when Pinky was followed by the drone in Central Park, I didn't take it seriously. I probably didn't tell you about that either. I actually thought it was kind of funny. It never occurred to me that it might lead to his death."

"A drone followed Pinky? That's odd. I spoke to Corey last night and he was pretty excited. He said there was a drone around his neighborhood for the last few days. He thought it was so cool. He'd never seen one in real life before."

"I've got to go."

"Where?"

"To Cor's house."

"In Queens?"

"Yes. You call him. Tell him not to go to his workshop today. Tell him to stay in and do not go near the drone. Tell him I'm on my way."

"What if he left already?"

"Leave a message. If he's not home, I'll try and get him at work."

Pushing me toward the door, Allana said, "Go, Ray. Go!"

I ran the few blocks to my truck. There were three large garbage bags and some beer cans in the bed. They weren't mine. The bags were wet and heavy. I threw them on the sidewalk and drove east to Woodhaven. There was a lot of traffic. Con Ed seemed to be working on every corner. The sound of a thousand car horns merged into one continuous howl.

Prepared to beg, I dialed Kazmarek as I drove. Voicemail answered, "Detective Kazmarek here. Leave a message." Fuck!

"This is Ray Lawson. We talked at the station. Remember? I told you about the drone in Central Park that followed Pinky Gold...I mean Stuart Goldstone—and then, *you* know, Stuart's car hits the base of an overpass on the BQE and—he's dead! Well, assuming..." I hit my horn. One of those low, matte black Dodge Chargers attempted to change lanes, aiming for the space my truck was occupying. I had to swerve hard to avoid contact. Jesus Christ! I continued my voicemail message to Kazmarek,

"Sorry, I'm driving and, whatever, it's not important. I called to say, my son is living in Queens, and he tells me there's a drone following him. I'm worried about his safety. Driving there now. Can you meet me there or send someone? Please! This is an emergency." I left my phone number and Corey's address.

I slowed down. A massive Peterbilt semi was backing into a loading dock. There was a long line of cars waiting for the truck to maneuver into the small space. It lurched forward, then backed up. Its air breaks squealed. Advanced a foot. Now back two feet. I waited patiently with the others. The big truck inched back. I put my foot down on the gas pedal and jumped the curb to the sidewalk. Horns blared, a lady in a Lexus gave me the finger, but I was free.

When I got to Corey's street, sure enough, there was a drone hovering in front of his building. The same kind of video drone that followed Pinky in Central Park. I parked and ran in, found 1C and knocked. "Corey, you home?"

The door opened. Corey said, "What's wrong Ray?"

I instinctively grabbed his shoulders then his arms, and leaned back to look at him. Looking for what? Injuries, I guess, but there were none. Corey was okay, just scared by my presence. "Nothing is wrong! Everything is great. I'm so glad to see you. I'll explain everything…" My phone rang. It was Kazmarek.

"Ray, I'm almost there."

"You got my message. Awesome. Thank you! The

drone's still here. It's out front, I think it would be best if you drive to the back of the building and come in the door that says Land House. We're in 1C. Okay?"

"Wilco, Ray."

I ended the call and looked at Corey, and said, "It's the drone. We think it might be dangerous. It's a long story. I'll explain soon."

Ten minutes later, there was a knock at the door. "Ray, it's me, Kazmarek." I slid the latch and opened the door. Kazmarek was carrying a shotgun. The policeman accompanying him wore full SWAT gear and had some kind of automatic rifle. Up close, he looked enormous. Kazmarek went right to Corey. "Hi son, I'm Detective Kazmarek, can I ask you a few questions?"

"Um, yes. Sure."

"How long have you been seeing the drone?"

"For a few days."

"Where have you seen it?"

"Here, a lot, and at the place where I work."

"Where's that?"

"Um, Jamaica Avenue."

"What's the intersection?" Corey looked at me.

"Cross Bay," I answered.

"Do you think it's following you?" asked Kazmarek.

"I just thought it was around a lot, but…I don't know. Maybe it's following me," said Corey.

"Ray, is it still out front?" said Kazmarek.

"Let me see. Yeah, it's still in the same place, around twenty feet above the middle of the street and directly in front of this building."

"You and Corey stay here. And stay away from the windows."

Kazmarek put a shell in the shotgun and pumped it. He left the apartment. The SWAT guy followed.

Seconds later, we heard a loud blast. The SWAT guy came to the door and said we could come out. There was a mangled drone and scattered debris in the middle of the street. The air smelled of gunpowder. People started to come out of the shops. Apartment windows opened. Residents peeked out to see what happened. The SWAT guy said to some bystanders near the splintered drone, "Hey folks, don't touch anything. Stand back, please." Around a dozen people, including Corey, were in the street, way too close to the splintered evidence. The SWAT guy walked over to the drone, put on rubber gloves, and placed the fragments in a plastic bag.

Kazmarek said, "These things have traceable serial numbers," I think we'll be able to find out who owns it. Could give us a lead on the Stuart Goldstone case. I wonder why anyone would want to spy on Corey, though. In any case, your boy should be safe now."

"Thanks, Detective. I really appreciate your help with this. Please let me know when you find out who owns that thing."

"Will do, Ray."

"Corey," I said, "I have a thought. Lock up the apartment, pack a few things, and leave a note for your roommates that you'll be staying with Allana and me for a while. You can go to work tomorrow if you like, or I can arrange for you to take a break for a few days. What do you think?"

"That sounds good."

"Excellent! And, later, I'll fill you in on the history of this whole crazy event."

"Good."

As he packed, I called Allana, told her all was well and that I was returning home with Corey.

***

On the drive back to DUMBO, Corey said, "That was exciting."

"Yes it was, wasn't it? A helluva lot more action than I expected. Detective Kazmarek doesn't fool around."

Allana was at the apartment when Corey and I arrived. She hugged Corey and said, "I heard you had a little adventure."

"It was awesome. The detective had a shotgun and we heard it go off and then we got to see the broken drone in the street," said Corey.

"Sounds like a movie."

"Yeah, like *The Terminator.*"

"Well, I'm so glad you'll spend some time with us. You know, we have to begin planning our Christmas party. We're gonna invite a lot of your dad's friends. What do you think about that?"

Corey said, "I like that." He went to the refrigerator, poured himself a glass of milk, and sat down on the couch. He pulled an iPad from his backpack. It turned on with a beep. He began playing a game with a perky electronic soundtrack. Jesus Christ—that's *my* iPad —the iPad I gave Corey when he and Fran visited for dinner. The drone wasn't following Corey, it was following my iPad. The damned thing was looking for me!

I led Allana to the bedroom and told her my theory about the iPad and the drone. "Now, that makes sense," she said, "that explains a lot."

"Nothing like this ever occurred to me when I gave Corey my iPad."

"Of course not! How could it? Will they be able to trace the drone?"

"Kazmarek said it could take up to a week, and no promises."

"Let's keep Corey here at least till then, Okay?"

"Absolutely."

19

Four days later, Allana, Corey, and I listened to the message Kazmarek left on my phone, "Hello, Ray. Bad news. The drone didn't show up on any data banks the NYPD has access to. I'm afraid it's a dead end. However, we think, with the drone out of commission, the operator's been warned. I expect you'll all be safe now. Just stay alert and notify me of anything unusual."

I ended the message and said to Allana and Corey, "Sorry, guys. I guess that's just the way things go."

"No, Ray! That's just unacceptable," said Allana. Can you get the serial number from Kazmarek?"

"I doubt it, but why would I do that? The police can't trace it."

"Because…I bet your friend Woody could trace that frickin' drone."

"Perhaps. Woody can go places the police can't, but I doubt that Kazmarek would release the number."

Corey took out his phone and said, "Look."

Allana and I circled Corey's phone. What looked like a pile of disjointed praying mantises was the splintered drone in the street in front of Corey's apartment.

"How'd you get that?" I asked.

"When I got close, I just snapped a few pictures."

"Nice work, detective Florian. Nice work."

"Oh yeah, well watch this," said Corey.

He zoomed in on one of the images. The serial number and other markings were quite legible.

"Any other tricks up your sleeve?" I asked.

"No, that's it."

"You did good, my man!"

"Corey, can you forward those images to me? I'm gonna put Woody on this and see what happens. You and Allana are geniuses!"

***

Just eighteen hours after contacting Woody, I received a package delivered by a bearded young man wearing a hoody imprinted with the words 'Valley Stream South Falcons XXL.' Included with the sixty five-page printout and jump drive, was Woody's handwritten note. Standing in the kitchen, I read it to Allana. "Tracing the drone was easy, a DJI Inspire 1 Pro Quadcopter, registered to a dummy LLC created by the New York headquarters of Anatolian Worldwide. Purchase date and origin are included in the enclosed material. Took the liberty of looking into Anatolian Worldwide. Hope I didn't overstep. Came upon an email server within Anatolian. A very secure Swiss system with end-to-end encryption. Nevertheless, I made entry. The account is used exclusively by Anatolian CEO, Peter Rademacher. When you read the email chains provided, it will be clear that Rademacher arranged for the drone surveillance, the murder of Stuart Goldstone, the abduction of Jeff, and a number of other unsavory things. All very damning. Please feel free to show this material to the police or make it public. Of course, no mention of me. - W."

Allana sat down and said, "Oh my God. What a relief."

"This is too good to be true," I said.

"We did it! We *really* did it."

"No, *you* did it. I was just gonna accept defeat."

"We all did it—you rushed to Corey's house and called Kazmarek. And how about Corey. Couldn't have done it without his photos. I'm just so relieved."

"Closure, sweet closure!"

I called Kazmarek and arranged to meet him at noon to deliver the packet.

"Allana, when I return, let's party."

"I'll be here, babe."

***

I got to East 67th Street right on time. Never noticed how beautiful the 19th precinct was. I knew it was a landmark, a

Renaissance Revival building, but today, with its sky blue window frames, it was simply glorious. Kazmarek was expecting me.

"So what've you got for me, Ray?"

I handed him the packet, "Just take a look."

He began to look through the papers. He nodded. He rubbed his shiny head. He grunted. He smiled. He nodded.

"Where did you get this?"

"It just appeared at my door."

"It looks real."

"Oh, it's real alright."

"How do you know that?"

"The gut. I feel it in my gut."

"Well, Ray, if this is what it appears to be, Rademacher will be arrested today. I can get a preliminary verification and a warrant in hours. Then we nab him. I'm not gonna miss this collar. Don't want to give him time to jump off to Switzerland or Brazil or wherever. When he's in lockup, I.T. can do a thorough check."

"I looked through the packet. It looks like there are instructions for hacking the encrypted Rademacher account. If you go there, your guys can confirm the authenticity of the information immediately," I said.

"Okay, Ray, it'll be best if you stay out of this now. But thanks for bringing the packet. It's dynamite, fucking dynamite."

"Well, my family and friends will sleep a lot better when

Rademacher is behind bars."

"We'll get the bastard."

"Before I go, I must thank you for all your help and for your quick response to my call about the drone."

"Just doin' my job, Ray, but I will tell you this—it was great fun blasting that drone. I hate those things."

"It was all very wild west. My son was impressed, and so was I. Thought you'd have to fill out forms with the FCC first and then get a court order or something, then maybe send a letter to the drone operator before you would be allowed to shoot it down."

"You might be right about the protocol, but I just wrote in my report that it dive-bombed me and had to be taken out."

***

I was at the stove flipping pancakes when the morning news came on. Allana was making coffee. I turned off the gas and put down the spatula. Rademacher was being escorted from Anatolian Worldwide's Wall Street Headquarters to a waiting car. It was iconic: Rademacher bent over to shield his face from the cameras, federal officers on both sides, gripping his arms. As one of the officers maneuvered Rademacher into the backseat of a waiting car, he put his hand on Rademacher's head and pushed down. Classic.

20

December 24, 2016

Allana and I arrived early. Savitha knew someone at Airbnb and snagged a DUMBO penthouse for the Christmas party. Allana was the event mastermind, but Nina and Savitha did all the grunt work. Savitha said most on the invite list were FOV's. I had to ask what an FOV was. Damn, I should have known that. Nina shouted orders to the guys setting up tables then went out on the roof deck to smoke. When she came back in she loaded a stack of Victor's CD's into the sound system. *Ghost Riders in the Sky* came up first. All decked out with strings of Christmas lights, the penthouse was looking good. The bar was set up, and platters of food from L'Artusi and Russ & Daughters were being prepared. Micah rolled in, and said, "Where the fuck is everybody?"

"Hey, Micah, so glad you came. It's a little early, but the bar's open. Get yourself a drink."

"Think I might just do that. I invited some other vets, Victor's friends. Hope that's copasetic."

"Copasetic, my friend, copasetic."

Allana and Savitha hung out by the door, greeting guests as they arrived. Speeches about Victor were forbidden, but Victor was why we all gathered.

The room began to fill. I saw some former grad students standing in a group, a guy in a classic motorcycle jacket and black leather pants, and some women who looked like models. I made my way to the bar, greeting students and old friends on the way. The bartender made me a martini. Someone grabbed the back of my shirt. I turned and saw Corey laughing. "Merry Christmas, Ray!"

"Merry Christmas to you." Corey's friend Fran was standing behind him. "And to you too, Fran. So glad to see you guys. You know there are a lot of friends of your dad here, Cor."

"I know. They've been kissing me too much."

"Yeah, that's a bummer. Here," handing Fran a napkin, "you can wipe the lipstick off his cheek. Did you guys see Allana yet?"

"Yes, she's so beautiful," said Fran.

"You're beautiful too. Now go get some food before it's gone."

I stepped outside into the cold night air to see if anyone was on the roof deck. A small group of pot smokers was sitting on chaises they'd arranged to form a circle. A young woman with a guitar was singing Joni Mitchell's "Big Yellow Taxi," but instead of the words 'Pink Hotel,' she substituted 'Trump Hotel.' I spied a familiar looking bald head. It was Kazmarek. One of Victor's vet friends was passing him a joint. Savitha joined the circle. The motorcycle jacket guy was doing a handstand on the railing at the edge of the roof.

Back in the penthouse, Allana danced with Corey. I danced with Fran. Nina was arm wrestling with Micah. There were a few burly dock-builders at the bar. I joined Crystal Breedlove and Robert Storr who were having an animated conversation with a tall elegant woman who just had to be a fashion model. She was saying, "…the history of art really makes more sense played backward. Place the Abstract Expressionists, the Dadaists, and all of today's young artists at the very beginning of the story of art and then proceed in reverse order to our revised terminus—the art of the Dutch Golden Age, the Baroque, the early and high Renaissance, for example. It's so simple, just put four paintings in a room—a Pollack and a Picasso, and a Vermeer and a Velazquez. Any viewer would have to admit, the Vermeer and the Velasquez, using pretty much any criteria, are more sophisticated and advanced—the inverse historical narrative is clearly more convincing. That's why Morandi, after playing with the modernists, decided to look to the methods of the past." The woman who spoke so eloquently and passionately, and who I assumed was some kind of supermodel, was actually Paola Orsini, a distinguished Morandi scholar from Bologna.

Wearing tee shirts emblazoned with the words "Kafka's

Kishka," some of Victor's former grad students circulated with two big trays of those legendary delights. They offered everyone a taste. Refusal wasn't an option.

Woody Redman rarely left his parents' house in Valley Stream, but he arrived with a picture-perfect chocolate cake his mother baked. I persuaded him, Allana, and Corey to pose for a selfie with me. The four anonymous musketeers who took down the mighty Rademacher!

Allana walked up six steps on the staircase to make an announcement. "Hello, hello my friends." No one heard her. The room continued to buzz with talk and good spirits until Micah's piercing whistle stopped everyone short.

"Miss Allana wants to talk," he announced. All eyes turned to Allana.

"Wow! Thank you, Micah. My dear friends, I just want to say a few quick things. First of all, this gathering wouldn't be happening without the hard work of Nina Spalding and Savitha Banerjee. Where are you?" Nina and Savitha raised their hands and everyone applauded.

"As you know, Victor didn't want any service or speeches, so we aim to honor his wishes."

"Ornery—even after death!" one of the vets yelled.

"Well, I don't know about ornery, but he certainly was opinionated—just one of the many reasons we all love him…but, enough of that. Thank you for being here tonight to celebrate his life and all the gifts he gave us—his art, his humor, his infectious joie de vivre, and best of all, his son Corey."

"Get up there Corey," yelled Nina.

Corey hesitantly made his way through the crowd, got up on the step with Allana, and to everyone's surprise, took an extravagant theatrical bow. The group went wild.

Allana said, "We have so much to celebrate tonight. Many of you know or *know of* the art collaborative called NoLab, if so, you probably heard about the tragic death of Jeff Goldstone's father and of Jeff's abduction. There were others threatened as well. As it turns out, a man named Peter Rademacher, the perpetrator of these despicable crimes, has been apprehended, and today we are all a lot safer. One of NYPD's finest, Detective Tadeusz Kazmarek, made a swift arrest, *and* our hero is here tonight." Allana pointed to Kazmarek. His eyes were bloodshot. He raised his hand to robust applause, and, as if holding a pistol, he pointed to the crowd and then from the elbow, bent his arm upward mimicking a recoil.

"I'm also thrilled to tell you, the two NoLab members who went underground are out of hiding and are here with us tonight." All eyes turned to Kaylee and Dave, and again there were hoots and applause. "I'm sure Detective Kazmarek's going to want to talk to them. Don't worry—they're ready. Now, one final thing." Allana held her hand out toward me and said, "Ray dear, please come here." I walked up, embarrassed. "Ray and I would like to wish you all merry Christmas, happy Chanukah, and a joyous

Kwanzaa. Stay as long as you like, dance, sing, eat all the food, and don't leave without trying the heavenly kishka."

***

The party slowed down around two o'clock. By three, the caterers were cleaning up. When everyone was gone and the penthouse still, Allana and I stepped out onto the deck. We held hands and shivered gently as little jetties of paper and dust swirled around us. The sounds of late night Brooklyn drifted up. The hum of the expressway, car horns, holiday music, barking dogs, distant shouts. Reflexively, I scanned the sky above lower Manhattan, searching hopelessly for the World Trade Center.

Acknowledgements

I am grateful to *NoLab*'s early readers for their valuable insights.

Special thanks to Gene Hayworth for supporting this project with patience and sage guidance.

CPSIA information can be obtained
at www.ICGtesting.com
Printed in the USA
JSHW031651120320
4695JS00002B/90